Jennifer Johnston

Truth or Fiction

headline
review

First published in Great Britain in 2009 by HEADLINE REVIEW
An imprint of HEADLINE PUBLISHING GROUP

I

Cataloguing in Publication Data is available from the British Library

ISBN 978 0 7553 3054 6

Typeset in Centaur MT by Avon DataSet Ltd,
Bidford-on-Avon, Warwickshire

Printed in Great Britain by Clays Ltd, St Ives plc

Headline's policy is to use papers that are natural, renewable and recyclable
products and made from wood grown in sustainable forests. The logging and
manufacturing processes are expected to conform to the environmental
regulations of the country of origin.

HEADLINE PUBLISHING GROUP
An Hachette UK Company
338 Euston Road
London NW1 3BH

www.headline.co.uk
www.hachette.co.uk

To the third and fourth generations
with love and high hopes

I work at home mostly at my computer, a newish Apple Mac, big screen, it didn't cost me an arm and a leg, but it looks very good. I am not very adept, a messy typer, but it does whatever I need, as long as no one asks me to do fancy tricks, those I can't manage at all. Anyway, the paper I work for accepts my copy without complaint, occasionally slight smiles, but that is all. If the machine stops working, or begins to behave badly, I throw it away and buy a new one. I have worked my way through four in my journalistic life. Letters I write with a pen; rather, cards I write, blue cards with my name, address and telephone number printed across the top.

Caroline Wallace, 13 Lansdowne Road, London W11, and, underneath that, my telephone number. I do not have a mobile or an email address. I like to keep things simple.

Yes, indeed I do.

I write book reviews and a few articles, from time to time, about esoteric and faraway places that no one really wants to go to; places with no tourist infrastructure, no swimming nor beaches nor, indeed, divine hotels with spas and all the sort of luxuries that the rich expect these days. These get published in very glossy magazines. I get paid a lot, but I have every intention of giving up this uncomfortable crap and buckling down to become a serious and thoughtful middle-aged expert on twentieth-century literature, and possibly also, if I live that long, twenty-first century literature.

I live in Notting Hill, that's west London, just in case you don't know. I have lived there for many years, since before that wretched film ruined all our lives, made us prey to gogglers and snoopers. I live in the top half of a pretty house owned by my cousin Rosie, who works in Geneva for the UN and is seldom home. I live happily there with a nice man who writes quite successful novels and in all the ten years we have been together he has never thought of asking me to marry him. I don't know why, and, perhaps stupidly, I have never asked. We are both getting on in years now, I am over forty and he is a few years more, so I don't suppose he will ever ask me. Maybe he sees marriage as a trap, a prison, a commitment in which he doesn't want to become involved, or perhaps it is just inertia on his part. I have waited hopefully for the past few years; I would like to have had a couple of babies, a dog and a cat. I had the confidence at one time that I could do the great womanly juggling act and cope with all that and my job, but that has leeched away with the years and now even the thought of babies, a dog and a cat leaves me breathless with exhaustion . . . and also a little melancholic.

Anyway, that's the way things were until about a week ago.

* * *

Caroline arrived at the office to find the telephone light flashing on her desk. The Lit. Ed. wanted to see her asap.

'Ah, Caroline. Good morning to you,' she said. She was staring at her over the tops of her glasses. 'Ever been to Dublin?'

'Dublin?'

'Dublin, Ireland. Used to be the second city of the Empire.'

She used to throw out useless bits of information like that from time to time. She pushed her glasses up her nose and stared at Caroline through the lenses.

'I know where Dublin is. I've never been there.'

'Ever heard of Desmond Fitzmaurice?'

'Umm.' Caroline thought hard and for quite a long time and the Lit. Ed. made squiggles on the paper in front of her with her pen. Finally, up through the murk came his name.

'Dead writer of plays, war correspondent, literary giant of the thirties. His war stuff was wonderful, I've read a memoir that he wrote.'

'Not dead. Very much, I have been told, alive. No one reads his books any more, no one puts on his plays, no one in fact knows his name, except, of course, the odd expert like yourself. I'd like you to go over and stir him up a bit. What does the old writer do when he stops writing? Or is he still writing? Is he a legend in his own country? Is he mad? Sane? Whatever. Go and find out. I believe he's about to be ninety.'

'Now? At once?'

'Why not? Why waste time? A week or so in Dublin ... God, I'd love it myself. Il Paradiso. But I am, of course, deskbound.'

She scratched the top of her head with her silver ballpoint.

'Nothing *tooo* serious, darling, a spot of gossip won't come amiss. I will not run the red pencil through a spot of gossip. After all, we're heading into the silly season.'

Her telephone rang. She waved a dismissive hand and Caroline left the room.

What to do? she wondered. What to do? Why has she picked on me?

This was not quite her scene; she stood in the passage fumbling in her bag. It seemed the right thing to be doing. When in doubt, fumble in your bag, most other women do it too. You are not alone. She brought out a pen and a small notebook and wrote Desmond Fitzmaurice on an empty page. Library, tel. no., publisher, tickets, and then a series of question marks. She snapped the notebook shut and threw it back into her bag and headed for the lift. No point in staying here. Must get this show on the road. Must tell Herbert.

She got off the bus outside the Odeon in the High Street and walked up through Holland Park. The sun was sliding down a bit towards the west, hitting the pale green leaf buds and shining in the windows of the stucco houses that backed on to the park. Some children still ran and kicked footballs on the grass and dogs snuffled round the roots of trees. In the woods a peacock cried. Even here the air was heavy with car fumes and bus fumes and, she thought, even the fumes from the planes streaking overhead. She wondered about Dublin. Rain; they always said it rained there, permanently.

Yiaoooo.

Should she write to him and ask him for an interview? He might not answer the letter. Telephone? Probably more sense.

Yiaooooo.

Peacocks. One of the wonderful features of Holland Park.

They could hear them from their house at night. Were they wailing for their demon lovers? Or just perhaps talking to themselves, reminding themselves of some terrible thing that had happened in their past? Bet you don't get peacocks in Dublin.

She came out of the gate and turned right towards the avenue. A frisky spring wind tweaked at her hair and blew dust around her feet. If someone blindfolded her now she would be able to walk home with confidence, right to the door. She knew every stone, every railing, every tree. She knew where the traffic lights were and the depth of the pavement edge and how many steps to cross the road. She knew the turn to Lansdowne Road, and each gate and driveway before she came to her own; she knew what each person grew in their front garden and each cat that sat on the wall, or lurked silently waiting in the long grass for unsuspecting birds, and she knew each tree, now coming into leaf, and the rustle that each one made as you passed it. This knowledge, she thought, is called love. The magnolia in their front garden had cream-coloured fleshy flowers which were just now uncurling themselves, showing off.

Caroline knew that Herbert was in the moment she opened the front door; she could hear his fingers pattering like rain on the keyboard. She couldn't do this, she had often wondered why; jerky spasms were all she could manage, a sort of Morse code of dots and dashes. Is it a lack of co-ordination in my fingers, she wondered, or a lack of co-ordination in my brain?

'Yoo hoo,' she called as she reached the landing, slinging her enormous handbag on to the floor. The pattering continued.

She went into the kitchen and switched on the kettle, it whispered for a moment and then sighed and then became silent. She wondered if she wouldn't rather have a glass of wine.

'There's some Sancerre in the fridge,' his voice called from the other room. Her mind was made up for her. She turned off the kettle.

He padded into the room. He ran his hand across the back of her neck and headed for the fridge. He never wore shoes or socks in the house. His feet were long and bony, skeletal almost, she thought.

'Today is the day for wine, not tea or coffee. I have finished the book.'

He opened the fridge door and took out a bottle of Sancerre.

'The end. Finis.'

'Darling, how wonderful. I'm so pleased.'

He groped behind him in a drawer for the corkscrew; it was one of those tiresome, very expensive ones that we all give each other for presents. He looked somewhat forlornly at it, before attacking the bottle.

'Twenty minutes ago I put that wonderful word at the bottom of the page and then I felt depressed.'

'Why on earth?'

'Two years' work and then The End. I felt cold and lonely the moment I typed that word. Look, my hands are shaking.'

She took the bottle from him and pulled down the two side arms. The screw sank into the cork with ease. Maybe the bloody thing was going to work this time.

'May I read it? Are you happy with it? Is it the best yet?'

He got two glasses from the cupboard.

'Tell you what we'll do. I'll finish my note to Angus. We'll wrap it up and take the blessed thing to Bloomsbury Square, drop it in the letter box and then go and have a terribly expensive meal. You can read it tomorrow.' He poured some wine into each glass.

She lifted hers and held it up towards him.

'To you, my darling, and the book and your successful future.'

'Ta ra,' he said.

Their conversations were like this quite a lot of the time, friendly, lazy, uncommitted. They seldom fought, or even argued, they were pleasant with each other. Yes they were.

* * *

Caroline found Desmond Fitzmaurice's telephone number the next morning without too much trouble and waited until ten thirty to ring him, not wanting to catch him in his pyjamas, so to speak. A cup of black coffee steamed beside her on the table. Herbert was singing in the bath, very loud and quite tuneless. It was a daft habit of his.

The phone rang and rang.

Shit, she thought, the bloody man is away.

'Yes,' said an angry voice into her ear.

'Can I please speak to Desmond Fitzmaurice?'

'No.'

'Well, when—'

'Who is it? What do you want? I can take a message.'

'I'd really like to speak to him.'

'No,' the voice said again. 'You can't do that. It is not possible. I have a pen. Give me your name and number and I'll get him to ring you back.'

There was a scuffling noise and a bang and the voice changed.

'Good morning, this is Desmond Fitzmaurice. Can I help you?'

Suave, smooth, well-oiled but old.

'My name is Caroline Wallace. I'm ringing from London. I wondered if it would be possible to come and see you. I work for the *Telegraph* and my literary editor would like me to do a feature on you, your plays, your wonderful war memoir, your involvement in Irish politics, all that sort of thing. A re-opening up of your life ... '

'A re-opening? What a perfectly splendid idea. I love the thought of being re-opened. By all means come and see me. As soon as you can or it might be too late. Ha ha, that last remark is a joke, just in case you didn't catch its tenor. Ha ha.' He chuckled away to himself. 'Come now. Come round this moment. Not much time to lose. I am almost ninety, you know.'

'Well, I'm in London actually, but I could come over tomorrow and spend a couple of days.'

'Do that. What was your name again? I forget things. Extreme old age, you know. Not to be recommended.'

'Caroline Wallace. I—'

'Caroline Wallace. I'm writing that down.'

She heard the scribbling of his pen. She heard the slight rasp of his breath.

'Yes, well, that's that. Give me a ring, or no, just come on out. I'll be expecting you some time tomorrow. It will be getting near to evening. Get a taxi. You work for rich employers, they won't begrudge you a taxi.' He laughed and rang off.

Her eye fell on a photograph of him taken many years ago that lay among his books scattered across her table. He was a handsome man, tall, dark-haired, with a long nose and a narrow smiling mouth.

Like someone?

Yes, like someone, but she couldn't think who.

Cary Grant? No.

* * *

Well, that was that anyway. She supposed she'd better tell Herbert, whose voice was no longer warbling in the bathroom. In fact, at that moment he came in through the door wrapped inadequately in a bath towel.

'I've been thinking,' he said. 'Well, for a little while, on and off and then in the bath, I just felt ... well ... why don't we get married?' He smiled at her. He stood there on the other side of the table and smiled, a lovely smile, warm, wonderful, just the sort of smile you need at a moment like that.

'Married?'

'Yes, darling. Married.'

'Why?' Caroline felt a huge anger beginning to grow inside her, an enormous, black rage spreading up through her body from her spleen or wherever it is that anger grows from.

'Why not?' His voice was cheerful.

'We've lived together for ten years without you feeling the need. Why now? I mean to say—'

'Book finished and it's good. I know it's good. The best. Wait and see. And then a prize. Marrying you would be such a prize.'

They stared at each other for a very long time. He began to look puzzled.

Words suddenly spilled out of her mouth.

'What the fuck are you on about? What does prize mean? Hey. Who gets a prize? Not me, that's for sure. I'd have married you ten years ago, in a flash, if you'd asked me, but you didn't. No, no. Let's move in together, darling. Let's be cool, trendy, no rings, vows, no carry-on, no church, no mothers-in-law, nothing like that at all. Don't you realise, you bloody prick, we could have had kids. Three or four kids, out there in the garden playing. We could have had all that wonderful hassle. I could have been a mother, not just a reviewer of other people's books. I—'

'Look here—'

'You talk about a prize. Oh God! I suppose you're starting to have twinges of arthritis. Have you been diagnosed as having diabetes? That happens to a lot of ageing men. I hear that around. Perhaps it's just normal wear and tear getting to you. Well, I'll tell you something for nothing. I have no intention of being anybody's unpaid nurse for the rest of my life.'

'You're being very unreasonable.'

'I am, am I?'

'I didn't know you wanted to have children. Why on earth didn't you tell me? I thought you were happy with me. I thought we were good together. I thought—'

'Just shut the fuck up.' She was going to cry. She could feel the tears boiling up behind her eyes.

'You are absurd.'

'Yes. I suppose I am. Very absurd. I hadn't considered the absurdity of my situation. Ten years! And now, in your idiotic bath towel, you say why don't we get married . . .'

'I'll go and put on some clothes. What would you like? What would be most suitable? A dinner jacket? Lounge suit? Jeans? Just say the word.'

The tears came, unstoppable, bursting out from her eyes. She put her hands up in front of her face to try and keep them under control.

'Shut up,' she snuffled.

'What?'

'Shut up.'

Gently he put the towel over her head, tucking the ends of it into her hands. He pushed her down into a chair. She pressed the towel to her face. She choked on tears, her nose ran. She was absurd. She knew that. He was right about that. They were both absurd. Is it possible to live a life that is not absurd? What did they talk about for ten years? Books, art, politics, gossip, food, where to go on holidays, never the way they should be living, never the nuts and bolts of life. No, of course not. They never bored themselves with such minutiae.

Caroline unwrapped the towel from her head and blew

her nose, and blew and blew. Absurd tears, absurd snot, her head was throbbing. He was no longer in the room. She wondered where he had gone. She got up and went over to the window and leaned her head against the cold glass. Below her in the garden the wind stirred the magnolia flowers. She heard the padding of his feet. He came back naked into the room, holding in front of him a cup of tea.

'A nice cup of tea.' He came over to her. She took it from his hand. She touched his face with a wet finger.

'God, you look awful,' was what he said.

She laughed. 'I thought you'd gone to put on your dinner jacket.'

'May I have my towel back?'

'I've blown my nose in it, pretty disgustingly.'

He twitched it from her hand and wrapped it round his waist.

'Snot a problem,' he muttered and then giggled.

Are we grown up or are we grown up? she wondered. We are definitely absurd.

She took a sip from the cup of tea. He was standing close beside her and put out a hand and wiped the tears from her face with his fingers.

'I really do love you.' He spoke the words softly. She felt the warm breath of them on her cheek. 'I can't think why I've been so churlish over all these years. I can't think why you've put up with me. I can't bear the thought that you might leave me. Please, darling Caroline, don't leave me. Maybe we never talked about the things that mattered, maybe we never will, but please, please—'

She remembered. 'I have to go to Dublin.'

He looked puzzled. 'Dublin?'

'Yes.'

'Ireland?'

'Yes.'

'Why on earth?'

'Work. I have to interview this ancient writer who nobody remembers and make everyone remember him.'

'Ancient?'

'About to be ninety.'

'Why bother?'

'She who must be obeyed. Stay not upon the order of your going but go at once. That was more or less what she said. So . . .'

She picked up the teacup and looked at the tea gently swirling inside it. It was not very nice. Herbert did not know how to make a nice cup of tea.

'The water wasn't boiling,' she said, putting the cup down on the table again.

'How long will you be gone for?'

'I don't know. It depends whether he has anything to say or not. He may be gaga, for all I know. He sounded OK on the phone. Rather pleased, actually.'

'Don't go.'

'I have to. I said I would.'

'Tell her you're getting married.'

'Am I?'

'Darling . . .'

'I have to go. I won't be away long and when I come back we can then discuss marriage, that sort of thing. Now go and put your clothes on. For once let's not be absurd. I want to go, Herbert. Maybe it will be an adventure. Can I live without you? Could I bear the thought that you're not across the landing in Rosie's spare room tapping away, or snoring beside me at four in the morning? I don't know. Can you live without me? Maybe you can. Maybe you'll flourish without me. Become a huge flourishing tree of a writer. For God's sake, man, I'll be back before you know I've gone. Go and put your clothes on and throw that snotty towel in the dirty clothes basket.'

They didn't say much more to each other that day and she went to Dublin the next morning.

* * *

The row of handsome grey houses had been standing there for nearly two hundred years, their facades protected from whatever hoi polloi might stroll along the terrace by wrought-iron railings, the gardens behind the houses sloping down towards the rocks and the unsleeping sea.

You'd have to love the sea if you lived here, Caroline thought as she stood by the door of the first house in the terrace, you'd never escape from that sound.

Breathing, sighing sound, peaceful at this moment.

Ssssh.

She pressed the bell.

She heard it ring somewhere deep inside the house.

Ssssh.

It was calm today, blue, patterned with sun sparks which seemed to float gently on the surface. It was licking with pleasure at the rocks below the lawns. Perhaps devouring, she thought, little by little, unnoticed, the rocks, the lawns, in time the houses.

Oh boy!

A slipway poked out into the sea from among the rocks and she wondered if Desmond Fitzmaurice had ever taken a little boat out from it, steering it south towards Bray Head, enjoying the gentle motion of the sea and hearing nothing but the mew of the gulls and the distant sound of the DART as it rocked along its track around the bay.

She put her finger on the bell once more. She was expected, she hoped she was expected.

'I am expected,' she said aloud

Of course, she thought to herself, you never really knew with old people. They forget things, appointments, stuff, they seem to forget a lot of stuff. They change their minds and don't tell you.

Tsk tsk. She clicked her tongue against her teeth.

Sssh. She wondered if the sea was laughing at her.

A black and white dog hurried down the terrace; it gave her a brief look as it passed by. She decided it had been up to no good.

I will count to ten and then I will ring again and after that...

The dog lifted its leg against the wrought-iron railings that divided the houses from the footpath, ran up two steps and gave a sharp bark. After a moment or two the door was opened and it ran indoors. With a click the door was closed again.

Oh boy, she thought once more.

She raised her hand to the bell. This time the door was opened immediately; a small angry woman was standing there.

'Yes?' She was wearing immensely high heels. 'I did hear you the first time.'

'I'm sorry. I—'

'Yes?'

'I have an appointment to see Mr Fitzmaurice.'

'Have you now?'

'Yes. I do. Caroline Wallace is my name. I spoke to him yesterday.'

'You did, did you? Well, I don't think he can see you now. He isn't well. He is not well.'

As she spoke she stared straight into Caroline's face with her huge pale-blue eyes. Malevolent eyes, Caroline thought. Truly malevolent.

'Wait.'

The door was shut in her face.

She wondered whether to press the bell once more or just stand quietly. She could hear the high heels tapping across the tiled floor of the hall. I'll wait, she decided; she could hear the sound of a door being crashed open and a high-pitched voice shouting. She couldn't hear the words, just the unfriendly tone of the voice. She stepped quickly to the edge of the steps and stared fixedly at the hill on the other side of the road; surprisingly, palm trees waved their long leaves in the wind, healthy-looking palm trees they were too, clumps of them, growing and waving cheerfully, as if they were on the edge of the Mediterranean, rather than south County Dublin.

Is this going to be a total waste of time? she wondered. Not just her time, but also the old man's time, even her literary editor's time. I should get a story of some sort, it may have to be a short story about standing on someone's doorstep in a foreign country; not much glamour, excitement or gossip in that.

I have to date seen one dog, some palm trees and a cross

old lady and listened to the sea below admonishing me, *ssssh.* The air smells good, better than London, no doubt about that, perhaps we should relocate. Yes. That bears thinking about.

The door opened. She turned and the old woman was standing there.

'He'll see you. Come in. Come. Come.'

Caroline Wallace stepped past her into the high hall. The floor was tiled with highly polished black and white slabs, and where the hall opened out they were covered by a red Turkey carpet. Light shone in from three open doors.

'This way.'

Caroline followed her.

The stairs to her left were wide and shallow and from the wall where they bent upwards an elderly benign gentleman gazed at her from an ornate gilt frame.

Courage, he seemed to say to her, don't let them perturb you, they are merely old. She gave him a brief nod and passed on through a door that the cross lady was holding for her into a high room with two long windows giving out over the bay. The walls were covered with books, floor to ceiling, and the mantelpiece was weighted down with photographs. An old man was standing, stooped slightly forward, by one of the windows, staring at the sea. He didn't seem to hear them coming into the room. A gull circled and circled and again circled and then dived into the sea.

'Oop la,' said the old man.

'Desmond.' Her voice crackled.

Slowly he turned towards her.

'My dear?'

'This is . . .' Her head moved slightly towards Caroline.

'Caroline Wallace. The *Telegraph*. We spoke on the phone yesterday . . .'

He moved towards her remarkably quickly, both hands outstretched in welcome.

'Miss Wallace. Of course. Miss Wallace. How nice to meet you. How do you do? I take it you have met my dear wife?'

'Yes. I . . .'

He took both her hands in his and swung them up and down. Up and down.

He had a soft grey moustache that swung up and down over his mouth as he moved his head.

'Miss Wallace.'

As suddenly as he had picked up her hands he dropped them.

She turned to Mrs Fitzmaurice and held out her hand.

'How do you do.'

The old woman pretended not to see. She walked across the room to the door, then turned to her husband.

'I presume you'll be wanting coffee?'

'Coffee. Yes. Coffee. How delightful. You'd like coffee,

I'm sure. Or perhaps you might prefer tea?'

'Coffee would be lovely, if it's not too much trouble.'

'No trouble at all. Is it, my dear?'

'What's trouble? And don't send her looking for it. I'll bring it in to you when it's ready.' She closed the door behind her as she left.

After a moment or two he said, 'My daughter, I don't know if you've ever met her, would say she's having a bad hair day. Young people say such odd things these days. She is not my wife's daughter. I have been married twice.' He turned his attention once more to the gulls. There were now ten or twelve of them diving and soaring. 'There must be a shoal of mackerel, they swim very close to the surface, you know. Sit. Do sit. Please.'

She sat at the big table and took a notebook and pen out of her bag. He remained silently by the window.

After what seemed to her like a very long time, he muttered 'Ooop la,' and turned towards her. 'I find this window fascinating, like a huge screen. So many things happen. Yes. Do forgive me. Now, what can I do for you?'

He crossed the room and sat down beside her. He gave her a very charming smile and sat quite still with his hands folded in his lap, waiting.

'Em . . .' she said.

'Are you frightened of me?'

'I don't really think so.'

'Young people are sometimes frightened of old people. It's not necessary, you know. I am not a frightening man. By no means.' He smiled at her again.

'I was trying to collect my thoughts. Trying to shove my inadequacies to the back of my mind. Anyway, I am not young. Alas.'

'Tut,' he said. 'Inadequacies. Rubbish. Whatever made you use such a word? Stupid inadequate things happen around the old, like not being able to tie their own shoe-laces or get out of the bath. Forgetting.' He became silent, staring inwardly intently. He nodded. 'I forget. My wife will tell you that. Nothing, of course, that is of importance. Why, anyway, should your mind carry stuff around . . . stuff that is unimportant? You should throw away words like inadequate.' He smiled at her again and leant towards her. 'I am a firm believer in throwing away redundant words . . . and of course in inventing new ones. Constant fluidity of language.'

'My editor asked me to come and interview you. She would like to bring you back to life again. She feels your work is too important to be let fade away, as it has. She would like me to reassess your work and also to do a feature on your lifestyle. How you live, how you have lived, the interlocking of your life and work.'

He was staring somewhat sombrely at her and she felt her face going red.

'Your, em, publishers seem to be very enthusiastic. She asked me to stress this.'

He put his hand up in front of her, like a policeman on point duty.

'If I understand you aright, Miss Wallace—'

'Please call me Caroline.'

'You wish to take the unimportant garbage of my life and stir it in with the important, with my work. You wish to make me intelligible to the masses. I never wrote for the masses to read.'

'Well, that's not exactly—'

The door opened and Mrs Fitzmaurice came in with a tray loaded with silver objects, cups, saucers and a plate of scones, thickly buttered.

He waved his hand towards the table.

'Thank you. Thank you, my dear. I do hope that is butter I see there, not that ghastly stuff they make in factories.'

She put the tray down.

'Of course it's butter, Desmond. You know perfectly well I wouldn't give you anything else. You also know what the doctor says. Will I pour?'

'Miss Wallace will pour.'

'As you wish.'

She turned and walked towards the door.

'Aren't you going to have some coffee with us?'

'No.' The word snapped out of her mouth like a pistol shot. She opened the door and was gone.

'She never does. She drinks neither tea nor coffee. They do harm to her nerves; that's what she says anyway. Do pour. Do please have a scone, butter or no butter.'

He reached out and took a scone and began to eat it. She poured and passed him the milk and sugar, neither of which he accepted. When she had settled herself down again with her coffee and scone, he spoke.

'Tell me how old you are.' His lips shone with butter.

'Forty-five.'

He stared at her and blotted at his buttery mouth with the back of his hand.

'Why do you ask?'

'I find it so hard to tell these days. I do apologise. From up here anyone under the age of fifty looks so young. You might have been twenty-three, a greenhorn. Why should I tell my secrets to a greenhorn? Hey? Answer me that.' He pulled a handkerchief from his pocket and rubbed at his face. 'I have plenty of secrets, you know, and if that's what you're ferreting about for I might just let you in on some of them. Forty-five.' He grinned a youthful and friendly grin at her and stretched out a hand and took another scone from the plate. 'We won't tell herself, Caroline. She fears for my health. She believes that with her help I will live forever. I do hope she's wrong.' He got up from his chair and went over to the window, chewing as he went. A large grey cloud had been blown across the sun and the room had become dark. She could hear his teeth clicking as he chewed. She wondered what he was staring at, the birds had flown off somewhere else.

'I indulge myself from time to time, when she isn't looking. That's a grade-three, low-level secret.' He turned towards her and pointed the scone at her. 'I like you.'

'Em, thanks,' she muttered.

'I will let you see my private diaries. I have them here. Locked. You never can tell who might be nosing around. Locked.' He pointed towards a large metal box in a corner by the window. There was a flamboyant lock and chain draped across it. 'From prying eyes . . . curiosity-killed-the-cat eyes. You will have to promise . . .' He popped the last bit of scone into his mouth. A trickle of butter ran down his chin. He rubbed at it with a finger. 'You must go away now. Have I got your number? You must give me your number. I must put them in some sort of order before you . . . a day, perhaps two. I will telephone you. We will make a plan. Um, yes. Write down your number for me.' He pushed a piece of paper across the table towards her. She ignored it.

'It was really only a couple of interviews . . .'

'Rubbish. Here I am offering to let you hear my tapes, read my diaries . . .'

'My editor—'

'Will be over the moon. This will be my life, rough and raw, as it was lived. Lots of sex and some violence.' He snapped his mouth shut and went back to the window. He breathed heavily as he stared at the sea.

'For years they have called me cold and grey. For years they have decided that I was dead. I don't suppose that any of my books are in print any longer. You can change all that. My future is in your hands. Need I say more?'

'But—'

'But me no buts, young woman. Have you written down your number? I am offering you an opportunity that you would be a fool to turn down.'

She groped in her bag for her pen and wrote down the telephone number of the hotel. 'It's in Ballsbridge.'

'I will be in touch. Soon. But you must promise not to breathe a word to her.'

'Who?'

'Her.' He jerked his head towards the door. 'Her. The banatee. She who thinks she must be obeyed.'

'What's a banatee?'

'The woman of the house. Gaelic. Not a language I speak, just the odd phrase here and there. Run along. I will be in touch. I feel quite buoyed up. The thought of a rosy future has cleared my mind.' He began to laugh quietly, his eyes fixed on the sea. 'Go, before I change my mind.'

She pushed the piece of paper towards the centre of the

table and got up. 'Don't leave it too long before you ring. I have to go back to London.'

He waved a hand at her.

She moved towards the door slowly, but he didn't say a word. He just stood there laughing quietly to himself.

There was no sign of Mrs Fitzmaurice. Somewhere upstairs Frank Sinatra was singing 'My Way'. She opened the front door and went out. The wind was sharp, and the leaves on the palm trees rustled. At the bottom of the steps she looked back and saw the angry face of the banatee glaring at her through the window. She waved at her and the old woman turned abruptly and walked away.

* * *

Later that afternoon the weather deteriorated; rain lashed down, almost obscuring the view of Bray Head and the Sugar Loaf mountain. Here and there tiny lights sparked in the darkness. The lights in his study were on; four wall sconces, the central chandelier, his table lamp and a standard with a big red shade just beside his chair. He was having his afternoon snooze, eyes shut, his head thrown back among the chair cushions, his hands clasped across his stomach. He had turned the chair towards the window, but there was nothing to see, merely the raindrops hurtling, racing, chasing each other down the glass panes.

He wasn't asleep; behind the soothing dark shutters of

his eyelids he was wondering how he was going to get to his Thursday rendezvous without getting soaked to the skin. That would mean stiff legs, sore back, shoulders useless for several days. A taxi, he supposed, was the only way. He hated the fact that nowadays, the Gardai having warned him about not driving his car, there was nothing for it but bloody taxis.

Bloody Phaeton would have to be called.

He nodded off to sleep for a few minutes and was awakened by her opening the door and bringing in his coffee. He kept his eyes shut and listened as she tiptoed across the room and put the cup down softly on a small round table close to his chair. She tiptoed back to the door again and sighed as she closed it. He knew what she would do next; she would climb to the top of the house where her sitting room was, settle herself on her sofa and read from her collection of Victorian girls' school stories. From time to time she would phone a friend and they would whisper secrets to each other for half an hour or so.

He pushed himself up in his chair and reached for the coffee. There was no point in letting it get cold.

Taxi. Yes, yes, yes. After he had finished his nap he would call one.

Phaeton.

Of course.

* * *

His Thursday rendezvous was with his first wife and he didn't feel like missing it, not on the back of a few drops of rain. They met in a pub halfway between his house and hers and would chat and laugh for about an hour or so.

She didn't know. Oh no, no, no, she did not. She would whinge and whine if she ever did find out and that would be too much to bear.

Pamela, his first wife, was four years younger than he was. That made her ... He frowned. Blast and damnit, did it matter what it made her? Made her old, no longer young. Yes. No longer young. She had managed to live her life without him, managed to still have laughter in her, which was more than could be said about this one here. Mind you, Anna used to laugh and joke, witty malicious jokes that brought the crowds around her. She had been a small twinkling person and she had loved him enough to do what he had wanted. That had been important to him. He was her be-all and end-all, like he had been Mother's be-all and end-all. Pamela had preferred her career to him; she had not been prepared to ... She had thought her life was as important as his. God! His mother had hated her. His mother had found holes in his socks one time when he had been staying with her and had railed against her. Railed. She had shouted at him. No woman should neglect her husband as she neglects you. And that dear little baby. When does she ever see that dear child? When?

C'était une bergère,
Et ron ron ron petit patapon.

She had a sweet soprano voice. It was a pleasure to listen to her.

C'était une bergère
Qui gardait ses moutons ron ron.
Qui gardait ses moutons.

I was her only love, he thought. Even beyond Father. Yes, to be sure.

He lay there in his chair with his head thrown back.

She used to whisper that to me. You are my only love. That is what we all want. To be someone's only love. We search.

His mother's voice rocked him to sleep again and when he awoke the rain had stopped and a strange ray from the sun hit the water below the house and made it sparkle.

Slowly he pushed himself up out of his chair and made his way to the door. He opened it a crack and listened. There was no sound. The whole house seemed to be holding its breath. He closed the door again.

Taxi?

Yes.

Phaeton. Yes. He would ring Phaeton.

Phaeton would be expecting a call. It was, after all, Thursday.

From where he was standing by the telephone he could see down into the garden; a man was pushing a lawnmower backwards and forwards over the grass. Sammy.

Sammy came on Thursday.

Winter and summer there was always stuff to be done in the garden. That was her area, flowers, planting, potting up, that sort of thing. As he thought about it, she came out of the house with a steaming cup in her hand; she was wearing a fancy apron and had changed her shoes for a flat pair of leather brogues. She walked across the grass and put the cup down on a sundial that was standing there waiting for the sun. Sammy turned off the mower and went over to her.

They would stand and talk, he knew that, about the dampness of the grass and whether it was too wet for him to be cutting it or not, about the moss on the steps that led down to the rocks. A steam hose was needed to deal with that. What was the name of the man who lived along the terrace, from whom they usually borrowed one? She would remember.

He reached out for the phone and dialled Phaeton. When he had finished speaking, he left the room, closing the door quietly behind him. He crossed the hall to the cloakroom, unzipped his pants and peed. Never miss the chance, he muttered to himself, squeezing out the last few drops. Never miss the . . .

Green hat, coat, walking stick, money. He patted all his pockets, yes, jingling and paper. He stepped out into the hall and opened the hall door a crack and stood there waiting for Phaeton.

✳   ✳   ✳

He sat in the dark bar of the Queens, a glass of whiskey on the table in front of him, around him a low rumble of male conversation. He liked that; no shouts or screams, no voices raised to the level where they penetrated your brain like buzz saws. A gentle rumble was good, soothing.

Pamela was late, but then Pamela was always late, she had always been late. It had been one of the things that first attracted him to her; the breathless laughter of her apologies, the flying hands as she spoke, the white lies, all quite charming. Until you had to live with it, that was, then it drove you wild with rage.

'Darling, I am s-so s-sorry. I do find time s-so difficult to cope with.' She would say it to directors, producers, writers, waiters; well, anyone for whom she was late, and her big eyes would quiver and she would be forgiven. She never arrived late on the stage, though, she could cope with time then all right. He felt exasperation rising inside him. Bloody woman.

He took a drink from his glass and pulled a book from his pocket. He found it more and more difficult to read nowadays, the words would begin to float from time to time, join up with each other and slide across the page; his mind also would slither from its thinking mode and play little tricks on him inside his head; but nonetheless, he still carried books in his pocket, this one, *Twilight of Love*, by Robert Dessaix, a short book full of secrets. He searched for his glasses in his pocket, but before he had time to fix them on his face he became aware of the small commotion, the displacement of air, that was Pamela's arrival. She was wearing a sand-coloured coat, wrapped well round her and tied with a bright blue scarf, which trailed down almost to her feet. Over her shoulder was a plastic shopping bag and on her feet a pair of old sand shoes, laced with string. Her face was gay and charming, though, her eyes sparking bright in the wrinkled flesh.

'Darling, I'm s-so s-sorry. The telephone rang just as I was leaving the house. I really must get one of those mobile ones so that I can talk as I journey. What's that you're drinking?'

He struggled to his feet, kissed the side of her face, soft and downy, and plumped down in his seat again, slightly puffed.

'Whiskey.'

'I'll have a gin and tonic.'

She began to unwrap herself, first the long blue scarf which she hung over the back of the chair, then the coat; underneath she was all in black.

'You look grumpy,' she said as she sat down. 'Darling, have you been waiting for ages? I am s-so s-sorry.'

'I should know by now.' He waved at a waiter. 'A gin and tonic, please.'

'Large.' She turned and smiled at the waiter. 'I've had a day of it. I need a purely medicinal large drink.'

'I hate old age, stiff and creaky, cranky, smelly . . .'

She took his hand and held it in hers. 'Would you rather be dead?' She ran her thumb up and down the back of his hand. He liked the feeling. He smiled.

'How can I answer such an idiotic question?'

'Just yes or no. There are times when I feel death would be divine, peaceful, silent, dark and then I shake myself and say no, I must go on living. Forever, forever. I love being a part of things happening. I was offered a part this morning. Imagine! Should I tell you? Well, yes, for a laugh. The nurse in *Romeo and Juliet*. I screamed when that casting lady from the Abbey rang . . . whatshername? Doesn't matter. No, I shouted at her, absolutely no. I haven't been able to remember lines for years. It's such a wonderful part, I can't say I wasn't momentarily tempted. Momentarily. Stupid woman didn't believe me. Well, she probably did really, but she made charming little sighing noises, mutterings, giggles. I put the receiver down. She won't ask me again in a hurry. How old am I anyway? You must remember. I never can. Everyone who really knew is gone. Isn't that a sad thing, Desmond? Are you lonely? Of course not, you have her.'

'Pamela...'

'I bet she knows how old you are. And me of course. To the minute.' The waiter appeared beside her with her drink. 'Dear man, thank you so much.' She raised the glass towards Desmond and then took a serious gulp. 'Oh God, that's good.'

Her hands had always been beautiful, he thought, even now, long long fingers and almond-shaped nails, painted red, sometimes scarlet, sometimes crimson, now at this moment a deep plum colour painted with great care, unlike her lipstick which was slipping sideways a little.

'Pamela...'

'Darling.'

'There is this young woman...'

'Darling, you're not doing that again. You're much too old.'

'I would like you to meet her. She works for some London newspaper and she's been sent over to do an article or two on me...'

'The *News of the World*, I have no doubt.'

'Don't be tiresome. They want to revive me. My

publishers wish me to be once more a monetary force. They are getting up off their backsides—'

'Me? Why me? Why should you want me to meet her?'

'You were part of my life.'

'An age, you silly man, an age, an age ago. You're not going to rake up all that stuff again. Youth and frivolity, all that sort .of thing. That before-the-war stuff? Are you? So boring. I can't remember anyway. I can't remember anything these days. Not just lines. Anything.'

'We had a child...'

'Oh yes. I remember that. I wouldn't go near her if I were you, with your young woman. She can be quite explosive at times. She considers you to be an old fraud. She might say that to—'

'Ellie and I get on very well together.' He sounded offended.

She giggled. 'Do what you want, but you have been warned. What age is this young woman?'

'Forty something.'

Pamela giggled again. 'Younger than Ellie. You are such an old goat. What does She have to say about this?'

'Anna doesn't know yet. I would like her to meet you. That's all, for heaven's sake. All the woman wants to do is write a couple of articles about me.'

She stretched out her hand and began to stroke the back of his hand again.

'I was startled when she told me what she wanted. I am yesterday's rubbish now. No one reads my work, no one puts on my plays, probably everybody thinks I'm dead.'

'Darling!'

'Perhaps they're right, I should be dead. I have outlived my—'

'Don't be an ass, Desmond. You're one of the greats. You know that.'

'No one,' he moaned. 'Fashion has swept me aside. Anyway, along comes this young woman . . .'

'Middle-aged' murmured Pamela.

'. . . and she wants to awaken the world again to my talent, she wants to say look, look at this man, this, this . . . Well, anyway, enthuse them once more, energise them. Good for sales, I thought. What do you think?'

'Absolutely.'

'You're mocking me.'

'Darling, of course I'm not mocking you. Why would I do a thing like that?'

'You always did.'

'You always thought I did. *Biiiig* difference.'

She moved her hand from his wrist; he missed the warm stroking of her fingers.

'Has she the stature?' she asked after quite a long silence. 'The gravitas, you know, all that stuff. It takes a genius to write about a genius.'

He smiled. He drained his glass and waved at the waiter. He held his glass in the air and twiddled it, then he pointed a finger towards Pamela. The waiter, used to such shorthand, nodded.

'Well, not quite a genius,' she said. 'I mean to say Leonardo da Vinci and Shakespeare were geniuses. Bach, Chekhov and Sam Beckett.' She stared into the space behind his head as if she were seeing each man whose name she mentioned. 'Piero della Francesca...'

'I get the message. Everyone doesn't think as you do. One man's genius may be a fool as far as another man is concerned.'

'Well, I'd like to know anyone who would disagree with the people I've mentioned.'

'Beckett? How about Beckett? I really hated *Godot*. So boring. And such bad jokes. Circus stuff. And you, I remember you used to fall asleep during Chekhov. I do remember that so well.'

'I always fall asleep while watching plays, that doesn't mean a thing. I've never fallen asleep on the stage. On the stage I have always been acutely awake. You know that well. I never wanted to stop acting. Not even to remain married to you.'

'Hunh.'

'Or anyone else. I do hope you noticed that I never got married to anyone else.'

The waiter put down two glasses on their table and took away the empty ones.

'Thanks,' said Pamela.

The old man said nothing.

'I've wondered why from time to time. Sometimes. Winter nights. They seem long and sitting by the fire watching television doesn't appeal to me all that much. And one's friends die. Pass on to some sort of glory. One less person to have a drink with or a good gossip. I could do with a husband then.' She giggled again. 'You could always push Her down the stairs and come and shack up with me.'

'Tut.'

'Actually, I presume you need looking after. I couldn't manage that. I hate looking after people. You would need meals cooked for you and buttons sewn on. All sorts of really boring things like that. Perhaps I'm better off as I am. Lonely occasionally.'

'My mother didn't like you. She told me not to marry you.'

'She preferred women who could sew on buttons. How did she get on with Her?'

'She was going downhill when all that happened. She was really unbalanced by my father's death. She didn't have the energy left to hate Anna as she had hated you. She adored the boys.' He stared across the bar, remembering how much he had loved his mother. *Elle fit son fromage et ron ron ron petits patapons.* I miss her adoration. Yes, indeed I do.

She had been a wonderful woman, kind, warm; she had believed in God. She used to sing hymns to him. He would sit on her knee as she played the piano and her sweet voice soared. *There is a green hill far away without a city wall, where our dear Lord was crucified who died to save us all.* Her dress was silk and her big breasts pressed warmly against his back. Her hands flickered like butterflies over the keys. *We do not know, we cannot tell what pains he had to bear, but we do know it was for us he hung and . . .*

'Where have you gone?'

. . . and . . . and . . .

'Desmond, come back.'

. . . and . . .

'I am not asleep.'

'I know you're not asleep, you've just gone somewhere else. Tell me more about this young woman.'

He took a drink. He thought for a moment.

'I don't know anything, except that she's here, in Ballsbridge.' He stopped. Why the hell should he tell Pamela any of this? He knew she had a problem with discretion. He knew she had a problem with laughter. He didn't need to be laughed at. He never had.

'I'd like you to meet her. That's all. You were a very important part of my life. You could talk to her about the

plays, that sort of thing. My early successful life. My ...
um ... engagement with post-civil war politics. The, um,
public reaction to my—'

'Oh, do shut up, Desmond. You can be such a pain in the
neck. She'll let me know what she wants. I'll give her my
version.'

'Very well. I can't expect more than that.' He sounded
wounded.

She remembered that wounded silence so well; it could
go on for several days, leaving her exhausted from banging
her head and her words against it. It had taken her several
years to recognise the fact that it had little to do with her
and it was best left alone. By the time she had discovered
this, it had become too late, their marriage had become a
broken thing, and the will to mend it had not been strong
enough in either of them. She wondered what would have
happened had she really fought when that idiotic baby thing
had happened with Anna. Her heart had not been in her
tantrums. Work had preoccupied her. She remembered that.
Was it *Troilus? Coriolanus* ... and the fool, Desmond, moping
around, muttering about doing the right thing by Anna. She
could have wrung both their necks. It was *Troilus* ... pretty
dismal play. Worth losing a husband for? She must have
thought so at the time. It was a principle, not a play. That
made more sense. Of course, in her heart of hearts she
thought he'd stick with her.

'I wonder,' she said, 'if we really loved each other. You and I. Perhaps we were like everyone else then, joyful messers.'

He laughed at her turn of phrase.

'We were that indeed. I loved you, though. We both wanted different things. Didn't we? I've never had much time for feminists and you were the first one that I had ever come across.'

'I wasn't a feminist.'

'Yes, by God you were.'

'I just wanted to act, to be in the theatre, direct plays. Feminism didn't come into it.'

'It was just the word you didn't know. It hadn't been invented yet.'

'I just couldn't understand why women had to toe so many lines. My mama never made me toe lines. She said I could do precisely what I wanted.'

'Your mama spoiled you to bits. When I met you, you were the most awful spoiled brat of a girl I'd ever met.'

'But you loved me.'

'I suppose I did. I thought you'd change. I thought that you would come under my wing, be a good wife and mother.'

'And boring.'

'I wanted to look after you. I wanted four children. I wanted a real wife.'

'The problem with you was that you only ever thought

about what *you* wanted. Me, me, me. That was all you thought of. Well, you got it in the end. I hope it made you happy.'

'Why do we meet? You are intolerable.'

'Because I entertain you more than She does. And I like to see the mess you've made of your life.' She paused for a moment and frowned a little. 'I don't really mean that. I like you. Probably more than any other man I've had in my life. We shouldn't have got married, but I still like you a lot.' She leaned forward, picked up his hand from the table and kissed it.

'Oh God,' he groaned.

'Let's be funny for a while,' she said. 'Let's tell each other funny and scurrilous stories about all the people we know.'

He drained his glass. 'I have to go, I'm afraid, my dear. I'm really sorry, but I must ring this girl, woman, or she may go back to London. That would not be a good thing at all.' He didn't wait for her to answer. He lumbered off across the room, leaving her with half a glass of gin and tonic on the table in front of her.

* * *

Caroline heard the phone ringing as she tried to open the door of her hotel room.

Probably bloody Desmond Thing, she thought.

It was one of those card things that you fit into a slot and pull out quickly, a green light flashes at you and hey presto your door opens. It never worked like that for her, though, and she longed for an old-fashioned key that turned in a lock. She flipped and fiddled and the bell kept ringing and then suddenly the green light shone at her and the door did open when she turned the handle, but by that time the phone was silent.

She lay down on the bed and stared at the ceiling.

Of course, it might have been Herbert. That would have been more acceptable. Much.

She wondered what it would feel like being married. Perhaps no different at all; but ... there was always the but. She thought of friends she had who had divorced quite acrimoniously after taking that step. Was it worth the risk? Did they really love each other or were they merely accustomed to each other? Was that enough to see them through?

She thought for a few minutes about high passion; the stuff of novels, of *La Traviata*, of *Romeo and Juliet*, the dreams she had had as a young girl.

I would have liked to have had children. I would love to have leaned out of the kitchen window and called out, 'Come in for your tea.' I would love to have held a child on my knee and a picture book, 'A is for apple, B is for balloon.' I would love to have a drawer full of school reports. Oh bloody fuck! Such sentimental thinking is a sign of old age.

Creeping old age. Now there were tears on her cheeks. Perhaps it was better to have someone beside you when that creeping started to happen. You could count your pills at the breakfast table, rub each other's backs, listen to the snorings and coughings, watch the dripping eyes, the shaking of the head ... oh, for heaven's sake, shut up!

The telephone rang again, startling her.

'Hello. Yes?'

'Darling.'

'Darling.'

There was a long silence.

She felt such relief at hearing his voice.

'Was your flight OK?'

'Yes. Great. No problems.'

'When will you be home?'

'I've only just arrived.'

'That's no answer. I miss you.'

She laughed. 'Good. I'm glad to hear it.'

'Do you miss me?'

She thought for a moment.

'I think so. Yes, of course I do ... you idiot.'

'When will you be home?'

'Soon.'

'Will you marry me?'

'Probably.'

'Yes or no?'

She laughed again. 'Bully.'

'I want to know.'

'Well, I can't say more than that. I met the man today. He's a little mad. He seems to be enthusiastic about me writing about him. He's going to ring me and we'll make plans. A couple of days, darling, that's all it will be.'

'I want to organise—'

'No. Wait until I come back. Please.'

'Will you marry me?'

'Herbert, I—'

'Why are you such a pain in the neck?'

'You're pushing me.'

'Oh, for God's sake!' He put the telephone down.

She held the receiver next to her ear for a few moments, listening to the purr and hoping that he would really be there, joking, laughing, being pleasant, but he wasn't. He had gone.

She looked out of the window at the neat landscape of the Royal Dublin Society, grass shaved, hedges clipped, paths swept and neat, not even, it seemed, a leaf out of place.

'I wonder what I'm doing here?' she asked herself aloud.

* * *

Desmond let himself into the house and shut the door quietly behind him. As he turned to cross the hall, she came out of the kitchen. She was wearing the rose-spattered apron that she had been wearing earlier in the garden.

'Just come in?' she asked.

'Ah, yes ... Yup. Just come in.'

'May I ask where you've been?'

'Just around. I've been for a little stroll.'

She looked him up and down, her eyes huge, amazed.

'You went for a little stroll?'

He nodded.

'In the rain?'

'It wasn't raining too badly. Just a little drizzle. Feel me. I'm hardly wet at all.'

He offered her his sleeve. She ignored it.

'Where did you walk?'

'I ... ah ... went up to the Queens.'

She laughed.

'Well, actually, George came and collected me in his car and he drove me home again. He didn't want me to get wet.'

'A kind soul,' she said and went back into the kitchen.

'Damn and blast,' he said under his breath. He opened the cloakroom door and threw his hat across the room on to its hook on the wall; it quivered for a moment and then settled. It was his only parlour trick and each time he did it these days, he held his breath in case the old hat landed on the floor. He then followed her into the kitchen. It was high and dark, a long time ago it had been the dining room, with a creaking, cranky lift that you rolled up from the kitchen, useless these days when there was no one in the kitchen to load and unload the damn thing, so they had divided the dining room in half and one side was a high and dreary kitchen, the other a high and dreary dining room. Dark, both rooms were dark. She was standing in the darkness by the cooker, stirring something in a saucepan. She was growing smaller and smaller as the weeks went by and he wondered as he looked at her if one day she might just disappear. *Phffft*, blown with the dust under the door, leaving only her high-heeled shoes behind.

He put out a hand and switched on the light, which dangled somewhat forlornly from a flex in the middle of the ceiling. It didn't make much difference.

'How can you cook in the dark?'

'I was afraid you'd be late for supper. They're showing *Little Women* on Channel Four. The real one, with Katie Hepburn. I was afraid I might miss it if you were late.'

'Drink?' he asked, opening the cupboard. 'Haven't you seen it about a million times?'

'G and T. Four, to be precise. Never tire of it. Never. Ice and lemon.'

As he mixed her drink, he wondered if he, too, was growing smaller. Stooped, yes, he knew that was happening. He could see from time to time his bent shadow on the wall when the sun shone through a window, or when he passed a shop window, he would see a stooped old man. Who is that stooped old man? he would ask himself and the answer always came, me, oh my God, it's me. Soon I will be smaller than my sons, he thought, her sons. Two small men, they took after her. They were quite cheerful, more cheerful than she was. She had been cheerful once. That had been a long time ago. He put her drink down on the worktop beside her. She mumbled something that could have been thanks.

He supposed it was his fault that she had become the way she was.

He wondered for a moment about Pamela and then poured himself a large whiskey.

'Sit down,' she ordered.

He took his glass over to the table and sat. He hated eating in the kitchen, but they always did when they were alone. Nowadays they were almost always alone. The boys came from time to time, some old theatre pals, now old codgers like himself, but usually when they entertained they would eat at the club. Food all right, not dazzling. Good wine and the view from the long low windows was quite wonderful. The harbour then the bay and across the evening sea the jewelled darkness of the hill of Howth. During the summer months, large yachts and smaller ones danced below them in the water, each one playing its own music as it bowed and dipped in the small waves. He would take

Caroline Wallace there. That would impress her, if nothing else. He supposed he would have to bring Anna. The thought made him groan.

'Are you all right?' Her voice sounded anxious. 'Desmond?'

'I'm fine, just fine.'

'You groaned.'

'Flatulence.'

'Or moaned, maybe.'

'I did not moan. And if I groaned it was, as I said, flatulence. I need to eat.'

'It's coming. It's coming.'

She took off her apron and threw it over the back of a chair.

'You have lipstick on your right cheek,' she said as she put his plate of food down in front of him.

Bloody hell.

He picked up his napkin and rubbed at his cheek.

'George's wife.' He muttered the words and then inspected the stain on his napkin.

She raised one daintily arched eyebrow and put her own plate on the table.

'I thought,' she said as she settled herself into her chair, 'that these Thursday drinking sessions were men only.'

'They are. She came to collect him. Kissed us all. Must have left traces on us all. Delicious fish. No one cooks salmon like you do, my dear. Yes. She kissed us all. Natasha is a very kissy lady. As you know.'

'It's tuna.'

'Ah.'

He watched as she carefully sliced a tiny piece of fish, a bird's peck, he thought to himself, and pushed it into her mouth. She had always eaten like a bird. Nibble, nibble, peck, peck. Once he had thought it was charming to sit and watch her. Why does love fly away? he wondered. He thought fleetingly of Pamela, her long fingers that she waved in the air as she spoke. She could have saved him from this if only she had done what he wanted.

'Eat,' she said.

'What?'

'I said eat. You said you were hungry, I give you food. Eat it.'

He picked up his knife and fork and began to poke at the food on his plate.

'You go into a trance sometimes. Or is it the beginning of something else? Something sinister?'

She spoke the last words with relish and then bending her head towards the plate took another bird's peck of food.

'I would like to know what the future holds in store for me.'

'Wouldn't we all, my dear.'

'I don't believe you care. Not about me, I mean.'

He chewed some tuna. He wasn't too keen on tuna, she knew that. He knew she knew that.

'I expect we'll end up in some charming and hideously expensive old people's home,' he said, 'surrounded by flower beds. You know, seasonal borders, always something in flower. Something for the old dears to look at. They'll give us calming potions so that we won't upset anyone by shouting or wandering about after lights out. The boys will come and visit us on Sundays.'

'Not funny.'

'It wasn't meant to be funny. I don't like to think about it.'

'The boys will make sure that we're all right.'

'The hell they will. Neither will Ellie—'

'Ellie!'

'She doesn't like me.'

'She'll grab what she can.'

'It's not a very nice dinnertime conversation.'

They ate in silence for a while; their forks scraped on their plates, the sound of their breathing was soft, the ice in her glass clinked as she raised it to her mouth, and outside, the wind blew up, pushing the clouds across the sky, covering the moon, the cars swished through the puddles on the road.

'There's this girl,' he said at last, pushing his plate across the table as he spoke.

'There is some pudding. I made a crème brûlée. Little individual pots.'

'That's nice. I like crème brûlée. Yes. Good.'

She got slowly to her feet. He wondered if she would make it or not. But he didn't rise to help her. She reached for the plates.

'Girl?' she said. 'What girl?' She picked up the plates and disappeared into the darkness at the back of the kitchen. 'Do you mean Ellie?'

'No.'

'Ellie is not going to put one foot into this house. That's my last word on Ellie. Dreadful woman.'

She came back to the table carrying two small dishes. Her ankle turned and she almost fell. He said nothing.

'Well, who then?' Her face was red and she panted a little.

He picked up his spoon and tapped on the top of the crème brûlée, as if he were opening a boiled egg.

'Not Ellie. The other one. The one who came earlier today. Caroline someone.'

'I remember her. What about her?'

'She's coming back again.'

'I think I will bring my pudding upstairs. I don't want to miss any of *Little Women*. You can wash up and put everything away. You will do that, won't you?'

He didn't bother to reply.

* * *

Caroline was washing her teeth when the phone rang. She spat and rinsed, swirled some water round the basin and went to the phone.

'Yes.'

'Caroline?'

She recognised his old scratchy voice.

'Yes.'

'Good. Are you all right? Have you eaten?'

'Yes.'

'There is someone I would like you to meet.'

'Mmm?'

'I thought tomorrow, that's Friday, am I not right? Yes, that's Friday. Well, three o'clock at the Queens. That's in Dalkey. That suits me and I suppose it suits you. I'll send Phaeton to collect you. No arguing please. The Queens is in Dalkey, right in the middle of the main street. He will collect you at half past two. That all right? I will of course pay. Then you can come back home with me and we can get down to brass tacks, and we will all have dinner at the club. That's a busy Friday organised.' He paused.

'Mr Fitzmaurice—'

'Desmond, please, Desmond.'

'Desmond, who is this person you want me to meet?'

He chuckled. 'Never you mind. She will have a point of

view. Warts and all, warts and all. Phaeton will pick you up at two thirty.'

'Who is Phaeton?'

'An old friend. He drives the chariot of the sun.'

He laughed.

He was gone.

* * *

He sat in his armchair by the window, no stars, no moon, only the lights rimming the bay and the cluster of light showing him where Bray was. His voice on the tape was lulling, he kept dropping into sleep and then waking with a little start.

'My word, my word,' he would say, his voice dragging him back to life for a few minutes.

Across a crowded room.

Such nonsense. Blithering nonsense.

I can hear Pamela's laugh away to my right. Chime of bells, I always think.

She, the woman whose face is fixed now in my mind, is listening intently to some man and I wish I were that man. Oh, how I wish I were that man.

Such blithering nonsense.

I concentrate my mind on Pamela's laugh.

Baby number one . . . asleep at home with Nanny . . . I have a question in my mind about that, but that has been overruled by Pamela. 'If you think,' she had said to me one evening as she lay feet up on the sofa, 'that I'm going to spend my days and nights looking after a baby, you've another thought coming to you. I was born to be a working woman. Remember that, old man, put that in your pipe and smoke it.'

She loves the child, there is no doubt about that. She plays with it, she tickles it, she boogie woogies with it and on Nanny's day off she takes it for a walk in the park. I don't know if she ever mastered the art of nappy changing, or ever will. I asked my mother this question once and she said, 'I doubt it very much.'

She does have this wonderful laugh. It tumbles endlessly through my head.

Ellie was the name of the child, after Ellie Dunn in Shaw's Heartbreak House, a part in which Pamela had been greatly successful. I wondered whether she would have a laugh like her mother. At the moment she just has a charming toothless smile.

The listening face on the other side of the room comes into my mind once more and I turn to look at her, to find that she is looking at me. She doesn't look away, just gives me a slight smile, then puts on her listening face again and turns back to the man who is talking to her. God, women are such bitches, I think.

I break into the conversation of the man standing next to me, Harry, Julian, Roger, yes Roger, Roger knows everybody. I nudge his arm. He turns slightly towards me, the words still dropping from his mouth. He frowns. He doesn't like being interrupted.

'That woman, with the hat and the red hair.' I nod in her direction. 'Who is she?'

His eyes flick towards her.

'Abby French. Painter. She's doing a line with Rory Beamish. A heavy line, just in case you have hopes. Har har.' He turns back to the man to whom he had been talking. 'Sorry, old man.'

I take a slurp from my glass and begin to push my way through the people who are separating us, leaving behind me Roger and Pamela's bell-like laugh.

I wonder what I'm going to say when I arrive, but I need not worry. She is waiting for me, her hand outstretched.

'You're so famous, I've been dying all evening to talk to you. You don't need to tell me your name. I'm Abigail French. Let's go and sit down somewhere.'

She tucks her hand into the crook of my elbow and we go together. She doesn't even look back and smile at the man to whom she had been talking.

'My word, my word,' he said. That's the way it had been all right. So long ago. He rubbed his eyes. That had all been so long ago.

Truth or fiction?

The whirr, the gentle clicks and the voice went on and he nodded into sleep.

Truth or fiction?

* * *

He had spent a lot of the night thinking about Abby, dreaming about her as he had done night after night all those years before. No other woman in his life, he thought, had been like her. Not even Pamela in the early days. He smiled. She was dead; her memory was varnished by that fact, her perfection would never fade. He sat in his chair by the window, watching the big clouds sailing across the sky, like galleons in full sail. He could hear Anna talking to the cleaning lady in the hall. She couldn't speak English but she would bow her head from time to time and mutter something incomprehensible, which seemed to keep Anna happy.

He switched on the tape machine.

It whirred for a moment, it clicked, it gave a little sigh.

. . . *she opens the first door they come to on the landing at the top of the stairs and pulls him into a dark room.*

'*Quick,' she is whispering in his ear. 'Quick, quick.' He starts to laugh. She pushes him down on to the bed and covers his mouth with hers. The stars are peppering the sky, shining through the big window. The bed is heaped with the guests' coats. She is fumbling with the buttons on his trousers. His breathing is short. What the hell is her name? Her mouth tastes of gin and nuts.*

'*Mmmm,' he moans. A soft moan.*

'*The moment you came into the room, I knew,' she whispers. 'The* moment you came into the room. Do you know what a coup de foudre is?' She giggles into his ear, warm breath, mmmm. She pulls his trousers down and settles herself on top of him.

He is drowning in overcoats, serge, tweed, silk, satin linings, silk scarves, and under his right ear a wonderful soft fur, smelling of animal. Wild animal... It must be, he thinks, the most expensive fur in the world. He snuggles into it. He snuggles into her. Mmmmm. Her hat is made of feathers and silk flowers. What the hell is her name? The hat jiggles on her curls. Nameless lady, I will love you forever. There is a sudden burst of music from the room below. He realises that he has barely touched her. There has been no exploration. He hasn't mentioned her nameless name. Her fingers are feeling his face, he catches them in his teeth, and after a while, having messed up several people's coats, they lie there in the still and quiet starlight, her fingers in his mouth. He starts to shake with laughter. She removes her fingers.

'You know, I can't remember your name.'

She giggles again and sits up and peers at him. Her hat is awry on her head.

'Abby,' she whispers. She kisses him, most tenderly, forehead, nose, mouth, and then pulls and pushes him up on to his feet. 'Go, go. We must not be discovered in flagrante delicioso. Button up, comb your hair. Oh lover, go. I'll see you downstairs. Ordered, we must be ordered by the time we meet again.'

He stumbles across the room and out on to the landing. The music is still playing. Before... before... he meets anyone, he opens door after door, no, no. The third one is a bathroom. He locks the door behind him

*and sits down, sighing with relief, on the loo. Across the room is a large
mirror. His face is covered with lipstick, everywhere. He laughs and laughs
and then, becoming calmer, he starts to wash himself.*

He laughs now at the memory. What unutterable hell it is to
be old, he thinks, farcical hell. Nothing in front of you.
Nothing at all. And what use are memories, or fantasies such
as these.

*   *   *

Caroline arrived early at the Queens, thanks to the prompt
arrival of Phaeton. A grey, unsunny man with a sharp nose
and bushy eyebrows. He hadn't spoken; he had merely
nodded in her direction as she climbed into his cab, and
nodded equally curtly as she climbed out again.

She sat herself comfortably in a corner of the large bar,
with a glass of red wine beside her, and opened her book.
The buzz of voices around her rose and fell, there was
laughter and the clatter of dishes, somewhere a TV
muttered on and on. The wine was all right, not earth-
shattering, but at least it wouldn't make you blind.

'Excuse me.'

She looked up. 'Yes?'

A woman was standing by the table. Old and young at
the same time. She had a purple scarf wrapped round her

head, out of which grey puffs of curls appeared; she held a pair of glasses in her right hand and was waving them in a friendly way towards Caroline.

'Are you waiting for Desmond?'

Her voice was what made her young, thought Caroline, low and slightly excited.

'I'm waiting for Mr Fitzmaurice. Is that who you mean?' She closed her book and pushed it to one side.

'Of course. Isn't it rude of him to be late. I'm usually the late one. My name is Pamela. He invited me to come and meet you. I can't think why. Some nefarious reason, I'm sure. May I . . . ?' She pulled out a chair as she spoke and sat down. She waved her glasses at the waiter. 'I hope you haven't paid for that.' She nodded towards Caroline's glass of wine.

'Well . . .'

'Don't. He has lashings of money, and, though I shouldn't say it, not all that much time left to spend it. He never splashed it around, believe you me, I know. Oh boy, do I know.'

The waiter appeared beside her.

'A large gin and tonic, ice and lemon, and another glass of red whatever. Decent . . . not the usual red ink stuff. Mr Fitzmaurice will pay for it when he comes.'

She put the glasses down on the table and Caroline saw that there was only one arm to keep them balanced on her face.

'And the house they live in must be worth millions. I suppose you don't know about Dublin house prices.' She rolled her eyes. 'Do tell me about yourself.'

'Well . . .'

'No, you'd better not. It might upset him if he thought I knew more about you than he did. Perhaps we should just sit in silence and sip our drinks. We could talk about our fair city, or house prices.' She began to unwrap herself from her long brown overcoat; underneath, she seemed to have a lot of fluttering coloured clothes, red, blue and green. 'One must keep warm when getting old. I used to be chic, very chic. That seems like about a hundred years ago now. Now I keep warm. Layers, they say, are the best bet. I have presses full of wonderful clothes at home. Never see the light of day. Sometimes I offer them to Ellie, but no. She refuses. Won't touch them. She prefers to buy her own clothes. "We are different shapes, Pamela," she says in a hoity-toity voice. Do you have children? I don't suppose you do. You don't have that slightly manic look about you that children give their parents as a sort of present. I suppose they're worth it. I have only the one. Ellie. She doesn't like me much and she absolutely loathes her father. Well, so she tells me, but I don't really believe her.'

The waiter arrived with their drinks and she gave him a most charming smile.

'They still have the odd Irish waiter here. Everywhere else they're foreign. Really foreign, not just Italian or French. They're Romanian, Bulgarian, Lithuanian, Polish, Russian.' She threw her head back and laughed. 'Who'da thought fifteen years ago that this private little country would be overrun with Lithuanians. Here he is. At last. Hello, my darling. You're the late one this time. I found your guest. It seemed too silly for us both to be sitting on opposite sides of the room, waiting. Just waiting and alone. I hope you don't mind.'

He bent and kissed her cheek.

'I heard you laughing as I came in the door. Miss Wallace, do forgive me. I am tardy.' He lifted her hand to his lips and kissed it.

'Please call me Caroline.'

'Caroline.' Pamela spoke the name slowly, staring across the table at her.

Desmond threw his hat and coat on to a nearby chair. He had a pair of gloves hanging round his neck on a long brass chain. He saw that Caroline was looking at them.

'I lose gloves,' he said pathetically, as a small boy might. 'Hundreds of gloves, all over the world. Pamela, Caroline. Caroline, Pamela.' He waved his hands in the air and the gloves danced. He fell into a chair. The waiter put a glass of whiskey on the table in front of him. 'That's the chap. Thank you, Sean.'

Caroline began to feel a little hot in the head.

'We've met,' said Pamela. 'I told her you were a tardy bugger. What I hadn't told her, though, was that you and I were once married. I am the mother of his only daughter. Would you like me to tell you why I left him?'

'Really, Pamela, I hardly think this is the time for that sort of thing.'

'You said you wanted me to tell her the truth. What I want to know is, your truth or my truth? That is the question. Is it not?'

'Don't be ridiculous, woman.' He took a long drink from his glass.

'We'll see.' She turned to Caroline. 'Are you going to write a book about him?'

'Good God, no. A few newspaper pieces. I'll reassess his work and do a couple of colour pieces. Stir up interest, that's all really. I haven't the courage or qualifications to write a book. Maybe someone else will, though. With a bit of luck.'

'With a little bit of blooming luck.' Pamela sang the words and winked at Caroline. 'You know I really think that I must pull myself together and write a book about him myself.'

'Pamela!'

'Shush, darling. Who knows you better than I? Warts and all. My biography of you would give everyone a great laugh.'

'You are a truly terrible woman. You never took me seriously.'

She stretched out her hand and touched his face. 'Yes, I did. You know I did. I took myself seriously as well. You never liked that.'

'I think I'll manage . . .' Caroline muttered.

'Pamela has always been a tease. You don't need to believe a word she says.'

'Come now, old man. Just be careful. You asked me to meet her so that I could talk to her about you. Did you not? You were a part of my life. You said that to me. Did you not? Oh yes, old man, you did.'

'I don't remember what I said to you.'

'Yesterday you said it. Your memory's a bit shot.' She threw back her head and laughed her beautiful laugh.

'I can remember perfectly well and I have all this stuff on tape. I'm going to play them to her. Play some of them. Yes, not all.'

'Portrait of the artist as a young dog. I bet that's one of your tapes.' Before he could answer she turned to Caroline. 'Where are you staying? Somewhere adjacent?'

'Ballsbridge. A rather posh place. My editor must have had a rush of blood to the head. It's not exactly adjacent though.'

'You must come and have dinner. Tomorrow. Yes. I won't ask anyone else and we can chatter on, warts and women and all that sort of stuff. Do say yes. I will be an invaluable help.'

Caroline looked at Desmond.

'She is up to no good. I should have known better than to rope her in.' He glared malevolently at Pamela.

'It's terribly kind of you—'

'A rat. I—'

'Don't talk rubbish, my darling.' Pamela got up and began to reassemble her outer clothing. 'I am a very good cook. It's the one domestic chore that I enjoy. You can come too, if you can escape from Her.'

He shook his head.

She giggled. 'That would be too much to expect. But anyway, it's best that she comes on her own, then I can exaggerate, illuminate, fantasise, with no one to say me nay. You'll come?'

'I'd love to. Thank you.'

Pamela began searching in her pockets, in the extreme folds of her clothes, in her capacious bag.

'I live in the most scrumptious house. It's like being in the country, down at the end of a long green lane. Where is my card? The taxi driver will know it. Every taxi driver in Dublin knows it. I don't drive myself. I have used taxis all my life . . . much, I may say, to Desmond's disapproval. Ah, here it is.' She pulled a card from a pocket hidden in the skirt she was wearing. 'I always carry a card or two, in case, just in case. Come about seven thirty. If you're going to bring me a present, don't bring flowers, bring a nice bottle of Bordeaux, nothing extravagant, Canon la Gaffelière, something like that, or a nice Pauillac.'

Desmond put his hand in front of his mouth and yawned.

Caroline nodded.

'There's a good wine shop in Ballsbridge, just near the top of Shelbourne Road. Helpful. You could mention my name, if you like.'

She whirled her brown coat around her shoulders.

'I must be off.' She held out a hand to Caroline. '*Au revoir. A demain.*' She bent and kissed Desmond on his right cheek. 'Good bye, my darling. See you next Thursday. I won't let her in on any extreme secrets, don't worry. Bye bye.'

She was away, flitting and stumbling through the tables.

Caroline put the card in her pocket. 'What a nice lady.'

Pamela turned at the door and waved at them.

'The problem with her was, she didn't want the same things I wanted. I humbly wanted a wife and family. There, I suppose, at my beck and call. I say humbly because it didn't seem to me that it was asking too much. It seemed to me to be what most women wanted. Comfort, safety, children, love. What do you say to that? My mother and father were a perfectly harmonious pair. Why could I not have that too? Hey? Harmony. After all, I was a most successful man.

Then. Yes I was. It is not too much to want harmony . . . but she . . .' His voice tapered off into silence, his eyes brooded back into the past.

'She didn't see things like that?'

He shook his head. He looked into his glass and swished the whiskey round. 'It was not a word in her vocabulary. She was a spoiled brat.' He took another big gulp. 'Even before we were married, I recognised that, not just spoiled by her parents but by her success. She was very successful. She loved herself. She loved me too, but obviously not in the way I wanted. I wanted her to become malleable. I thought that when the baby came, Ellie, that she would see the way ahead. It was so clear to me.'

'Your way.'

'In those days it was everybody's way.'

'What a closed little world you must have lived in.'

He stared at her for a long time and then shrugged. 'I might have known you would not understand. Anna understood. She became the woman I wanted. It's all to do with the weight of your love. In Pamela's scales, the theatre won. Hands down. I was an also-ran. I never wanted to be that. Have another drink?'

'Oh no thank you.'

'I did not want to be known as Pamela's husband.'

'I can see how that would have been very irritating for you.'

He finished off his drink and plonked the glass down on the table with finality. He leant towards her.

'Tell me, what music do you hear in your head?'

She was mildly startled. 'No music. I don't hear music in my head.'

'Rubbish. We all do. We all have music or songs, sometimes they come quite unbidden and stay for hours, maybe just a phrase which recurs over and over. It is there willy nilly, at the back of our thoughts, our conversations. Our life moves to its rhythm. Sometimes we burst into song, without intending to. The words just spilt out of our mouths.'

He paused, he scratched at the side of his nose with a finger.

'My mother was a piano teacher until she married and she had this little book of songs for small children. It was called *The Baby's Bouquet*. I used to sit on her knee and she would play them for me. She had a very sweet singing voice. I can remember nearly all of them. German, French and English. I still have it at home. She sings them in my head from time to time. That I find most enjoyable.'

He cleared his throat and looked expectantly towards her.

'Well . . . umm . . . I sing those French songs to myself. I have no voice, so it's only for myself. You know. *Rien de Rien, La Vie en Rose*, that sort of thing. *La nostalgie*. The French are so good at it.'

He laughed and clapped his hands. 'Three cheers for *la nostalgie*. That's good. I like to think of you singing those songs in empty rooms, or on the tops of mountains. We might become friends. Pamela's OK, you know. She really is. A decent woman. She'll probably tell you some silly things. We should have stayed together. I think that from time to time. But you know how impetuous youth is. I never thought ahead. She didn't want me to change my ways, become a different person. No. That would have been one of her strengths. She was a spoilt brat, though. Difficult to live with. She was the youngest of five. No discipline. A rough and tumble sort of upbringing she had. She called her mother Mama, I called mine Mother. What does that say to you?'

'Not much. I called mine Mum.'

'Mama has a certain ring to it that I like. She was a great lady, Pamela's mama. She was Irish ladies croquet champion. Tall and golden-haired, like a valkerie might have been. Pamela laughs like her, a beautiful hearty laugh, like bells ringing in your head. She never left this country and yet she seemed to be familiar with the whole world. No, that's not quite true, when her second daughter was married she went to Holyhead . . . on that awful boat.'

'Why on earth . . . ?'

'Mixed marriage. No priest in Dublin would perform the ceremony, so they had to go to Holyhead to find one who would. They do things differently over there. But I think that little trip put her off foreign travel. Anyway, you see how times have changed here. Our own boys call us Desmond and Anna. Ellie . . . doesn't call me anything at all. Probably bastard inside her head. She sees me as seldom as possible. I'm talking rubbish. I recognise that. I am spewing. I must be nervous of you.' He stared at her for a very long time, making her also feel nervous. 'You have a very closed and private face. I don't suppose you ever do anything as stupid as spew. Do you?'

'I try not to. I believe to a certain degree in composure. I like to keep control of my behaviour.'

'Well, well. Bravo. Maybe you are the woman I should have married. All those years ago. Maybe for you I would have toed the line. Ha! I see by your face that you find that unlikely.'

He pushed his glass to one side and struggled to his feet.

'We must get back to the old witch and her spells, her potions and incantations. I always get the feeling if I don't toe the line she'll turn me into a barn owl. *Tu whit tu wooo.* Would you hold my coat for me, please? I am neither flexible nor supple any longer. A cause for sorrow, believe me. We have Phaeton outside. He waits in all weather, the driver of the sun's chariot.'

He adjusted the brass chain and clapped his hat on his head and was off across the room, waving and bowing as he went. At the door, he took her arm.

'This evening, my dear, we will dine at the club, just the three of us, and you can interrogate Her. But for now, home, James.'

A taxi was waiting at the door, its meter ticking. Phaeton got out on to the path and bowed mockingly.

'Sir. Madam.'

'I always sit in the front. As I said, I am no longer flexible or supple, so forgive me.'

He hopped most flexibly into the front of the car. She climbed into the back and Phaeton closed the door.

'As I said, home, James. Home is where the heart is. Home is where you hang your hat. Don't spare the horsepower. You, of course, remember Miss Wallace from earlier. Caroline, my dear, this is my good friend Phaeton. Years of knowing. He drove me through the war. In one side and out the other. Both unharmed. Untouched by bullet or bomb. We were each other's guardian angels. We called his jeep the Chariot of the Sun. Written across the—'

'Would you put on your seat belt, like a good chap. Then we can get going.'

'I can't. I can't,' muttered the old man irritably. 'The damn thing doesn't fit me.'

The driver leant across him and pulled at the strap.

'I tell you it doesn't fit me.'

'And I tell you it does. Breathe in for a moment. And I also tell you that if it doesn't go on, we don't go on. You can walk home, so you can. All the way.' He tugged again and it clicked. 'There you are. It's better to be safe than sorry. Now you can yak away to your heart's content.'

'Seven o'clock. That's when we will need you next. Seven. We will be taking this young woman to dinner at the club. Then you can collect us at ten thirty and after you've left us at home you can drop Caroline to Ballsbridge. There you are. It's all organised. No problemo.'

'If you would sit at home with your good lady and not be gallivanting out in the rain and shine, you'd have no problemos.'

'And not much fun either. You must remember, Phaeton, that even the old and pretty incapacitated need their fun. Would you not agree, my dear Caroline?'

'It seems to me that Mrs Fitzmaurice doesn't get much fun.' She felt brave saying those words.

There was a little chuckle of laughter from the driver and silence from Desmond. He turned round and looked at her.

'She takes what fun she wishes. No one would stop her doing that. She has a lot of friends. She and they congregate from time to time. They go to the theatre, the cinema, to tea shops for rich and creamy cakes.'

'I'm sorry. I didn't mean to be rude.'

He smiled at her in a forgiving way. 'It can be quite

melancholy to be old. One of the most aggravating things is the way the past keeps slipping away from you. Happenings, triumphs and failures fade. People's faces fade. Even the most dearly loved ones.' He sighed deeply.

They drove in silence for the rest of the short journey.

By the time they arrived at his house, pale grey fingers of fog had started to stretch across the street. Phaeton stopped with a jerk and then reached across Desmond and pushed the door open. Some lights in the house were shining. Desmond pulled a bundle of notes from his pocket and shoved them towards the driver.

'I expect I owe you more than that, but that'll do for the moment.'

'Excuse me,' Caroline's voice made him jump, he had forgotten about her presence in the back of the car. 'Is this club posh? I mean, should I not dash home and change. I have a tidy—'

'Yes, yes, yes. By all means. Phaeton will drive you to the hotel and wait for you. Don't hang about, though.'

He was out of the car and up the steps, jangling his keys in his hand, before she had time to say anything. At the door he turned politely and took off his hat to her, she waved and then Phaeton drove off through the strips and stripes of shifting fog.

* * *

'Abby was the love of my life.' He whispered the words to himself as he disrobed in the cloakroom. He threw his hat and it quivered and landed on its hook, giving him a little jolt of pleasure.

The lights were on in the top of the house, shining down the stairs, and he could hear the chattering of the TV.

'I should have married Abby. How stupid I was.' He closed the study door behind him and switched on the light. Outside the windows, the sea and the fog were intermingled, it was impossible to tell one from the other. The garden looked as if it had been inundated. The mist swirled in his mind, streaks blurred his thoughts. He couldn't work out why she had come at that moment into his head; if she were to walk through the door at this moment, would he recognise her? He groped in the mist for her face, but Ellie's came instead. He remembered intensely the night he had told Ellie about Abby, how he had longed for her, bled internally for her. She had leant across the table and poked him in the chest with her fork.

'Serve you bloody well right.' Then she had laughed. Laughed!

'What on earth did you leave Pamela for? And me? Why did you go? I may only have been eight years old, but I was old enough to feel pain and loss and terrible loneliness. And I couldn't understand why. I was always expecting that you would come home. Every time the doorbell rang I thought it was going to be you. No one told me that you had gone forever. No one gave me that bit of information for five years. So I have the right to laugh when you say you pined for whatsername. And I don't understand why you're telling me all this rubbish now.'

'Your mother and I were incompatible.'

'Puh.'

'I gave her everything she wanted. All the freedom . . .'

'Puh.'

She despised me, he thought, I could see that in her face. I can see it now in her face. I was telling her my truth and she despised me for it. I had wanted sympathy, little cries of sadness and understanding, her warm hand touching my cheek. And what did I get? Puh! And of course a moral lecture. I hate this fog. I hate not being able to find things in my mind when I want to. I hate the intimations of mortality. He sat down with a thump into his armchair. I hate the ghosts that flit, yes, flit in and out of my consciousness.

He leant forward and flicked on the tape machine.

Out past Kilcoole they floated, rocked by the waves, warmed by the benign sun. The tide had turned on them when they had been unconscious of it and now the coast of County Wicklow was slipping away.

'Holy God!'

He grabbed for the oars and began to row. He had never rowed naked before and it felt faintly ludicrous. She lifted her head above the side of the boat and began to laugh.

'Where, o Theseus, is the minotaur? Where is Orpheus and his lute? Where, o Desmond, king of rowing men, are we going to end up?'

'Holyhead.'

'I do hope not. It's not my favourite place. How about Mount Parnassus?' She laughed again. 'You do look funny. Your sweet willie flips and crumples as you row. Here.' She threw him his pants. 'Cover it up. You might do him some damage . . . Bloody hell, mine have disappeared.' She was searching round. He leant on the oars and watched her. God, how scrumptious she looked.

'My knickers,' she wailed. 'They're not here. They must have fallen overboard. They must be on their way to Wales. Maybe some fisherman will catch them in his net and think they belong to a mermaid.'

'Do you think that mermaids wear knickers?'

'These ones, for sure. They were the most beautiful in the world. Seduction knicks. Seven pounds fifty in Brown Thomas, bought specially to seduce you . . .'

'And I never even saw them.'

'What a waste of money. Next time I won't wear any.'

'How do you know there'll be a next time?'

'Because I'll die if their ain't.'

She watched him row for a moment or two.

'You do love only me, my darling, don't you?'

'Only you. In all the world of sky and clouds and glorious sun. Only you.'

'What about Pamela?'

'No more Pamela.'

'What about . . . anyone else?'

'Darling, what a question!'

She raised her eyebrows at him. A little warning pulse throbbed for a moment in his forehead. She smiled at him, her eyes drifted down from his face along his body. He felt the prickle of their touch as they moved slowly.

'Mr . . . ah, Beamish?'

She shook her head. 'I believe in monogamy. I really do. Rory got the push the other week. He did. Believe me, his poor heart was broken. I think he may have gone to join the British Army. There is going to be a war, you know. We haven't had much time to talk about that sort of thing.'

'No. Things will change, though, my darling.'

'Soon?'

He shipped the oars and stretched out his arms towards her. Damn the tide. Damn Wales. Damn, damn.

He admired the sound of his own voice, the slightly flat vowels and the nasal sound of the consonants gave him pleasure as well as the memories they conjured up.

The door opened. His finger pressed the stop button.

'Yes?' His voice was disgruntled, no longer charming.

'You said you were bringing that girl, woman, back with

you. Have you changed your plans? I thought we were going to eat at the club. There is no food for dinner in this house.'

'What woman are you talking about?'

'Sometimes it seems to me you're going very like your mother.'

'My mother?'

'Yes. Your poor dear mother. She got very forgetful towards the end. If you remember.'

'She was ill. Very ill.'

'Caroline someone.'

'Ah, yes. She went home to change. She felt she was not appropriately dressed for the club. You are right about the club, my dear, we are eating there. No need for you to get in a state about food. She should be back in plenty of time. I'm sure she would appreciate a drink before we go.'

'I'm sure she would.'

They stared at each other. Then she moved her eyes towards the tape machine.

'What were you listening to?'

'I wasn't listening to anything.'

She raised her eyebrows and began to whistle a strange, discordant tune. She turned and went out of the room and walked up the stairs, the sound of the whistling trailing after her like a long crêpe de Chine scarf.

I hate these little skirmishes, he thought. He picked up the tape machine and put it in the metal box. You never know. She could come in and snoop around, listen to his secrets. If she had not already done so. Indeed.

Life wouldn't be worth living if she studied his secrets. No. No. No.

His mother's voice sang soothingly in his head. Sweet and clear, each word like a little chiming bell.

> *There was an old woman as I've heard tell.*
> *She went to market her eggs for to sell.*
> *She went to market on a market day,*
> *And she fell asleep by the king's highway.*

He used to stand beside her and turn the pages, and her charming plump fingers ran over the keys and her rings sparkled and she smiled at him as she sang.

He sat down in his chair and put his head in his hands. Her love had been all around him. Nothing, he thought, nothing had ever been like that again. That total safety. That total adoration. He drifted into unwanted sleep, accompanied by the sweet voice of his mother.

> *Along came a pedlar, whose name was Stout,*
> *And he cut her petticoats all round about.*
> *He cut her petticoats up to her knees,*
> *Which made the old woman to shiver and sneeze.*
> *Shiver and shiver . . . and . . .*

Somewhere a bell rang.

His mother's voice faded.

Shiver and . . .

He opened his eyes.

The mist was pushing against the glass, trying to get in.

The bell rang again and he heard Anna's footsteps crossing the hall.

He rubbed his eyes, he pulled his hair straight and struggled to his feet. He smiled a welcoming smile.

'Miss Umm,' announced Anna.

'Please call me Caroline. Good afternoon again, Desmond. Except perhaps I should say good evening.'

He moved slowly towards her and took her hand.

'I paid the driver myself. He didn't want me to but I insisted. I'm just letting you know in case he puts it on the bill.'

'Which,' said Anna from the doorway, 'he will do. The man's a robber. Like his father was before him. That is, if it was Mr Costello, which I presume it was.'

'I don't know his name.' Caroline became aware of the fact that Desmond was stroking the back of her hand with his thumb. 'What was it you called him?' She removed her hand.

'Phaeton. Greek, of course.' Anna seemed to be enjoying herself. 'He drove the chariot of the sun. Still does, I suppose. Round and round. Eternally on and on.' She waved her small hands round and round her head. 'Never use a simple name like Mr Costello if you can use a Greek alternative. That's right, isn't it, Desmond darling? Now, how about drinks for us all? I'll go and see to that.'

'Can I give you a hand?'

'I can manage to cope with drinks.'

She was gone.

'Won't you sit down?' He waved his discarded hand towards a large comfortable chair.

She took off her coat and scarf and looked around for somewhere to put them. He took them from her and threw them over the back of one of the chairs that stood round the table. She sat down, her back to the window and the mist, and waited to see what would happen next. He walked over to the window and stood there, frowning slightly.

'My mother never saw this house, I mean the inside. The whole terrace is very visible from the beach. In a way the whole terrace rules the beach. She was dead long before we bought it. She died during the war, you know. She used to worry so much about my... well, safety. I sometimes wonder... whether... Once a week she used to write to me, little snippets about her daily life and of course what was going on in the city. Anna and the elder boy lived with her for a while. A couple of years. There didn't seem to me much point in them sitting in London being bombed. Anyway, it was company for my mother and Anna was able to work. She wouldn't have been able to work in London. No. Arthur, yes, Arthur loved his granny. And I think she loved him. I think she liked boys better than girls. All my old toys were there, up in the attic. She had never given any of them to Pamela. She had them all stored neatly away: soldiers, a train, even my old blue teddy bear. What do you think?'

'What do you mean, what do I think?'

'Is this sort of domestic stuff any use to you? Any interest?'

He turned his chair and settled himself down into it so that he could look at her face, his long thin legs stuck out in front of him. She noticed for the first time that he was wearing fleece-lined bedroom slippers and his ankles were bare and heavily lined.

'I wonder what Pamela thought?'

He laughed.

'She hated it. Absolutely hated it. There was Anna, under her very nose. If they crossed the street, they bumped into each other, metaphorically, you understand; Anna was the mother of the son and heir and they were both in the same business. Dublin was too small for that to be comfortable for either of them. I was amused. I sat out in the desert and laughed when I thought of them, their spats and skirmishes, and of course cried when I thought of how I had lost Abby. You see, the moment Anna told me she was pregnant, I knew I would have lost Abby. I knew that glorious part of my life would have to be over. I had to see Anna right. Back in those days it wasn't like ... well ... wasn't like ... so I laughed in Cairo, and in Italy and Austria, and mourned and wrote and broadcast about the war, led a sort of *Boys' Own Paper* war ... That's the way it is: Heroism, Tragedy, Comedy, Cowardice, Hatred, Love ... God, all those capital-letter words we throw at the public, so that they don't realise the horrible squalor of the whole damn thing. *Boys' Own Paper*. I was good at that stuff.' He knotted his fingers for a moment and fell silent, then with an effort he pulled himself together again.

'It was over then and I rescued poor Anna. I brought her and the boy to London. She seemed happier there.'

'And you?'

'The bloody war was over, that made everyone a lot happier. I wrote well then. I think you would agree that my best plays were of that period. Being out of this small pond had a very liberating affect on me. I was not the only one who benefited from that freedom.'

There was a bump at the door and Anna's voice called out something.

'Yes, yes.' He struggled to his feet. 'Coming, my dear.' He stamped across the room and opened the door. Anna came in carrying a tray clinking with glasses and bottles.

'Now, isn't that nice. We were just talking about my postwar plays. Umm . . . Caroline agrees with me that they are the best. Honed, would you say that they were honed in a way that the earlier ones were not?'

'Well . . .' Caroline began, but was interrupted by a short laugh from Anna.

'Such bilge you do talk,' she said as she put the tray down on the table. 'Now who wants what?' She looked at Caroline and waved a hand towards the tray. 'Drinkies, my darlings. Personally, I am having a gin and tonic. What about anyone else? A modest Scotch for you, Desmond? Pour it yourself, but make sure it's modest. We don't want the doctor tutting at us. And you, Caroline?' Her hand fluttered over the bottles like a demented butterfly. 'What can I get you? Desmond, modest was the word I used. That is an immodest whisky. You can't take your eyes off him.'

'Is that white wine? That's what I'd really like. I'm not much of a spirits drinker. Thank you so much.'

They held their glasses up in front of them and silently toasted each other.

'My mother . . .' began Desmond.

'Your mother spent her days sitting in a comfortable chair and people did things for her. You did. I did. The maids did. Everyone in her life did exactly what she wished. You have always been obsessed by your mother.' She turned to Caroline and gave her a very charming smile. 'He has always been obsessed by his mother.'

86

Desmond returned to his chair and plonked himself into it. He took a large and rather noisy gulp from his glass.

'Are you staying, my dear? If so, do sit down. We will all be uneasy if you hover around like that.'

'No. No, no, no. Never fear. I have to go and tidy up and before I do go, I must say to you, you may not go to the club in your bedroom slippers. You may wear them to your rendezvous in the Queens, but the club . . . no. That I will not tolerate. I will knock on the door fifteen minutes before Mr Costello arrives and you must tidy yourself up, comb your hair, wash, put on shoes and socks. Spruce up.' She left the room.

'I am not, nor have I ever been obsessed with my mother. I am shocked that Anna should say that I was. She didn't last long enough to see me safely home from the field of battle. That was such a sadness. She would have been so pleased to see me come in the door, safe and sound. I used to dream about her. Yes, indeed I did, in Italy. Night after night, her long grey hair blowing in the north Italian wind. She wanted me home then and of course I couldn't go and so she died. Just went. Killed, I would say, like so many others, by the war. Those dreams were surprising to me. I had never had dreams before, and her blowing hair, that almost shocked me. Neither had I ever seen her hair loose before. It was always so neatly netted and pinned, but there it was in my dream, always, always the same dream, she just sat there and the cold wind blew her hair this way and that and she called my name, but I was imprisoned by the war and couldn't move, not even an inch, towards her. I couldn't hold her hand or touch a strand of her blowing hair. I would wake up then and shout bugger Hitler, bugger Churchill, bugger Roosevelt. Bugger them all. Not out loud, you must understand, inside my head I screeched. Then one day I got a telegram to say that she was dead and the dreams stopped. Just like that.'

He sighed and stopped talking.

The mist had retreated and Caroline could now see the grey waves curling and uncurling at the bottom of the garden.

His mournful voice began again.

'I got home the day before the funeral and almost the first thing I did was ring Pamela. I wanted to bring Ellie to the funeral and the moment I knew what the arrangements were, I rang. She was after all my mother's eldest grandchild. Pamela was adamant. Venomous, I thought. I thought it was a perfectly reasonable request. I would collect her and bring her home. Personally, I thought that Pamela should have come too, but I knew she wouldn't. She was, as I said, adamant. Adamant.' He closed his eyes and pondered on the word for a while. Caroline sipped at her white wine and wished that she were in Notting Hill.

'Adamant. Venomous. She was very difficult in those

days. Yes. I was in no mood for a row so I just let it be. I banged down the receiver, if my memory serves me right. The sound of her voice grated the inside of my head. I was already exhausted and deeply stressed. Deeply. I can't tell you how . . . well, just weary from the war and then on top of that losing my dear mother. I just banged it down.' He took a handkerchief from his pocket and blew his nose. 'Banged it down.' He looked across the room at her. His anger evaporated.

'Why should I burden you with my ancient problems? Silly irrelevancies, or maybe you might not think they were irrelevant. How can I know what you will think?' He leaned forward and pressed the button on the tape machine again. There was the usual whirring noise and then his voice.

I am so sick with love for you, I can't think. I can't work. I can't read. Your face gets in the way.

'Darling Desmond, where are you?'

'At home. In my study. My hand holding the phone is shaking. My head is shaking because your voice is in my ear. Are you a witch? What sort of spell have you cast on me, you beautiful, wonderful witch?'

'Will I come to you, on my broomstick?'

'No, no. Pamela is here, in the next room.'

'Then you must come to me. Now. Come at once. I can't wait to see you, to have you here with me.'

She puts down the receiver.

'Abby,' he calls. 'Abby, Abby.'

He gets up and runs to the door. He can hear laughter and a murmur of voices. He runs and runs.

He switched off the machine and looked towards Caroline. She frowned slightly.

'I don't know what all this is about,' she said. 'It's fiction, isn't it? Pretty ghastly fiction. I mean to say.'

Behind him the mist had come down once more, thick grey curtains and the darkness of the evening.

'It sounds to me like fiction.'

'You can take it from me that it is memory, not fiction at all. Memory.'

'When did you tape this? How long ago?'

'I work at it all the time. It is living in my mind. Day after day, another memory sweeps into my mind. I have to tape it in case it . . .'

'What?'

'It disappears and I would be left with nothing. I could be left without her. For years I was without her. The inside of my head was full of blackness. Pour me another drink, there's a good girl. Bereft is the word I have to use. For years I was bereft, a shadow, no one saw me, spoke my name, no one read my books. I sometimes wondered if I had ever existed. My mother had died and then Abby died and there was no one left to love me any more. No one to know who I really was.'

'I am confused,' said Caroline. She handed him his glass. 'I don't understand why you didn't marry Abby. If you were going to leave Pamela and marry anyone else. Why not Abby?'

'Ah,' he said. He took a sip from his glass, he held the drink in his mouth for a moment or two and rattled the liquid round, then he swallowed it. 'Ah,' he said again. He shut his eyes. She wondered if he had fallen asleep or if he was trying to remember all that way back into his past, or just trying to get his fiction straight. She could hear Anna singing to herself out beyond the hall ... I want to be loved by you, boopy dooo, only you, nobody else will doooo, boopy doo ... and then a slithering sound as if she were dancing by herself around the hall ... boboopy dooo. You, you, you. Nobody else will ...

He had fallen asleep, his head drooped down towards his chest and a little drool of saliva ran from a corner of his mouth. She sat, lonely, and sipped at her drink.

'Yes.' He spoke suddenly, making her jump. 'Memory feeds us. Not only our own proper memory, but also our folk memory, our ... our ... "old unhappy far-off things and battles long ago". The sleeping tiger, there in all of us. Waiting to spring, pinion us to the ground with memories.

Smother us. What do you say? What do you think? Hey?
Girl.'

'You've been asleep.'

'Resting. That's all. Being old is not very nice, you know.
Untoward things keep happening. I could live for another
twenty years, you know. Isn't that a frightening thought?'

There was a blast of dance music from the radio. Loud
and then softening down to a murmur, strict rhythm, Victor
Sylvester maybe.

'Twenty unproductive years, being a bloody nuisance to
people. What the hell is that woman doing? Is she dancing?
That's probably what she's doing. We used to dance a lot.
Between the wars, recovering from one and forgetting the
horrors and waiting for the next. And of course we had our
own wars right here. Right here. We danced through them.
The only thing to do. They all danced well.'

'Who?'

'All of them. All the women I loved. I danced well too. I
used to glide with aplomb. Pamela won a silver spoon for
ballroom dancing once. With a chap called Theo something
or other. He was plump. Together they did a very neat
foxtrot. She laughed so hard about that. We all laughed. She
probably still has that spoon. That was, of course, before the
war. We had all stopped our laughter by the time the war
came.'

'But you weren't there when the war came.'

'I suppose you're right. I wasn't with Pamela. No. That was over. Over. But I was coming backwards and forwards. I was with Anna and the boy in London until the bombing started, then I brought them back to live with Mother. Anna's family were upset about the baby, but Mother never said one ugly word about him. I think she was so relieved that I had left Pamela that . . .' He became silent once more. 'I wonder sometimes if we were really quite inconsequential. If we still are. What do you think?'

Anna drifted into the room on a tiny skiff of music.

'Time's up,' she said. 'He'll be here soon. Desmond, come along. Now.'

He stood up. 'Ah yes. Phaeton will be with us soon. Anna, my dear, will you show Caroline the cloakroom and I will go upstairs and order myself. Shoes. Hair. That sort of thing.' He marched with confidence across the room.

As he passed Anna by the door, she put out a hand and patted his arm tenderly, squeezed his grey gnarled fingers.

* * *

Perhaps, she thought as she lay tucked into her bed, just perhaps everything was going to be OK.

The foghorns moaned insistently. She would never get to sleep.

She tossed and turned. She wanted to ring Herbert and hear his friendly voice, but good sense prevailed. She dozed rather than slept and the foghorns moaned. It had been a charming place to eat, down on the very harbour's edge, the staff had been friendly, the food good. She was sure that on a normal evening the view was magical as they constantly described it to her, across the harbour and the sweeping bay to the hill of Howth, all strung with lights and the lights of steamers as they moved across the black water, but that evening they had been bandaged in by fog, unable to see anything except their own reflections in the windows of the dining room.

Anna had pushed her food petulantly round her plate with her knife and fork.

'Is your dinner not to your liking?' Desmond had leant across the table solicitously towards her.

'It's simply delicious,' she snapped back at him.

Polite conversation had almost come to a standstill.

'Are you married?' Anna asked her.

'Not yet. I—'

'Keep your freedom. It is such a precious thing. You never realise how precious it is until you've lost it.'

'My dear, you jest. She jests, Caroline. She has all the freedom anyone could possibly want.'

'I neither jest nor joke. Pamela was right. She wanted freedom. She left you.'

'I beg your pardon, my dear, in case you've forgotten, I left her. She kicked up a rumpus. Surely you remember that?'

'How could I ever forget it?'

The lamb cutlets were pink and tender, tasting of garlic and herbs. Caroline chewed, her eyes fixed on her plate.

'Should I tell Miss . . . ummm?'

'Her name is Caroline.'

'Should I tell her about Pamela's rumpus . . . at least one of her rumpuses? Should I?' Her malicious eyes sparkled.

'I don't—'

'My version. The true version. Before she hears that bitch's version.'

'Really, I—'

Anna turned to Caroline. 'You must realise that Ireland then was not like Ireland is now. By no means. Then we wallowed, no, we drowned in sin. Now we revel in it. Then we were tormented by fearful guilt, Protestants and Catholics alike. We all clung to our own true cross, begging for forgiveness, crying out to be saved.'

'Do get on.' Desmond whispered the words half under his breath.

'I was much younger than she was. Much. I was barely more than a teenager. And talent. I did have talent, didnt I, dear?'

He looked blankly out of the window into the fog.

'He was like God. So tall and handsome. He still is handsome. You must admit that he is handsome?'

'Oh yes. Of course.'

'I was playing Puck.' She stretched her hands out in front of her, fingers spread wide.

> *Now the hungry lion roars,*
> *And the wolf behowls the moon;*
> *Whilst the heavy ploughman snores;*
> *All with weary task fordone.*

'The Dream. You know. Rushing, flying, a wonderful hermaphrodite character, neither man nor woman, a slave. I was dressed in leaves, nothing else. I just seemed to be leaves blown by the wind. "I am sent with broom before, to sweep the dust behind the door." I chanted and whispered, now you hear me, now you don't. She was one of those quarrelsome ladies.'

'Hermia.' He whispered the name.

'He used to come, if he wasn't doing other things, to collect her in the car after the show. They might go and eat, go to a party, or maybe go and dance somewhere. We were all mad about dancing in those days. Sometimes he would stand in the wings and I would notice him watching me. From time to time a breeze would blow across the stage and my leaves would flutter.'

Her eyes glittered with the memory and she glanced across the table at him; he continued to stare out of the window.

'Act three, I rework my spells. Presto.

Jack shall have Jill,
Nought shall go ill,
The man shall have his maid again,
And all shall be well.

'Off I go.' She clicked her fingers and waved her hand merrily in the air above her head.

'I stumbled as I ran past him and he put out his hand to stop me from falling. No plan, I promise you. I really did stumble. And I just stood there leaning against him and my heart was beating and I felt so happy. I knew at that moment. He knew too. Didn't you, Desmond?'

He shifted his eyes from the window. 'Didn't I what?'

'That time in the theatre. You knew.'

'So long ago.'

'Anyway, after the curtain had come down that evening, Madame Pamela shouted at me across the stage that I should leave her husband alone. "I saw you," she shouted. "I saw his hands flittering through your leaves. Oh boy, yes I did." Someone laughed and she took off both her shoes and threw them at me and left the stage. She was immoderate. Her whole family was mad, weren't they, darling? Quite mad.'

'I was not aware of it.'

'That was just a bit of a rumpus, by no means the biggest or the best. Just a trifling one. I could tell you—'

'I don't suppose this is of any interest to Caroline. I think we should talk of other things.'

Which they had of course done, shoes and ships and sealing wax and cabbages and kings. This is not my scene, she thought, these are not my people. I am homesick. She laughed at that. She snuggled further down under the bedclothes. I can laugh at them, but I don't like them. I feel no sympathy for them. I want to go home.

Home, moaned a foghorn. *Home, home.*

The mist crept in her window, wrapped round her bed, the sound of the foghorns would keep her awake all night.

All night, all night, they moaned. *Home.*

Bloody hell, she thought, how can I sleep? How can I . . . how . . .

* * *

Desmond and Anna were in the hall; he stood drooping, dejected, central, under the Venetian chandelier, while she locked and double-locked the front door, twisting the large key and fastening the chains and bolts. A safety measure, she called it; he called it paranoia. He took off his green hat and dropped it on the floor.

'What do you think of her?' His gloves and their chain were next on to the floor. 'I do . . .' he was struggling with the sleeves of his overcoat, '. . . not like her. Not. I do not think much of her. Why did I take her to dinner? Answer me that.

Nobody understands me. There is no one left.' He threw his coat on to the floor. A little dribble ran down his chin. 'I shall resign from that club. I have said it before, but this time I really mean it. And I won't see that woman, whatever her name is, again. I don't care what the publishers say. I can't be wasting my time . . .'

She picked up his hat and reached out for the chain holding the gloves.

'Don't be silly, Desmond. You liked her before and you'll like her again. You've had a spot too much to drink. In the morning you'll feel differently. And you won't resign from the club, you know that full well. Away with you, upstairs to bed. A good sleep is what you need.'

'You're treating me like a child.'

'You're behaving like a child.'

'Pamela never—'

She hit him with his hat. 'Don't mention that bitch to me. Never. Never.' She hit him with his overcoat. She threw his gloves at him.

He clenched his fist and raised his arm.

She began to shake before his eyes.

'Don't hit me,' she wailed.

'Don't be such a bloody fool. You're not worth hitting.' Slowly he put his arm down and turned towards the stairs. 'Poor white trash.'

'Desmond!'

She began to run after him, but her feet became entangled in his coat and she fell, hitting her head on the tiles.

'Desmond!' It was a scream. He was running from her up the stairs and did not look back.

'Jesus. Jesus. Jesus.'

The words reached after him as he ran.

* * *

Caroline was awakened by the telephone.

Herbert, she thought, as she stretched out her hand.

'Darling.' Her voice was heavy with sleep.

Wrong.

'Come out here at once. Something's happened.'

'Desmond?'

'Of course. Get a cab.'

'What time is it?' She squinted at her watch. 'It isn't even half past six.'

'A cab. Come out at once.'

'Hang on a tick. I'm in bed. I was asleep. What's the matter?'

'I'll pay for the cab. Just come. Please. Something's happened to her. Something terrible.'

'OK. I'll be there. I'll be as quick as I can, but it will be at least half an hour.' She put down the receiver and lay back into her pillows, looking at the ceiling. The fog had cleared and the shadowy branches of trees undulated gently, lit by the rising sun.

What can possibly have happened?

Why didn't he ring his sons?

Or the doctor?

Or some friend?

Why the hell me?

She picked up the phone and rang Herbert.

No reply.

No reply.

Angry and very disgruntled, she got out of bed and went into the bathroom and turned on the bath taps; the water spurted out in a neat arc. Just looking at it calmed her down a little.

* * *

She rang the doorbell and after a few moments she heard his footsteps shuffling across the hall. He fumbled with the chain on the door, he undid the locks, he swore at Anna's careful securing of the house. She tapped her foot with impatience. At last he opened the door a crack and peered out at her. He appeared to be toothless. He recognised her and opened the door for her to come in. He was in his pyjamas and a somewhat grubby dressing gown, tied around him with a long tasselled cord. He smiled at her. He was toothless.

'Here I am.'

Carefully he closed the door behind her.

'Yes. I didn't know whether you'd come or not.'

'You sounded a bit desperate.'

'Did I?' He frowned. He wondered why she had used that word. Had he sounded desperate? Had he been desperate? Why? What was desperate?

'Desmond . . . why did you ring me?'

He remembered.

'I think she may be dead.'

'Who?'

'She . . .' He shuffled his feet. 'You'd better come. She . . .' He turned and went back across the hall, followed by Caroline. 'Her. Anna. She's much heavier than you would imagine. So I had to pull her . . . I put her, well, she was cold. I couldn't leave her on the floor. No. Could I?'

She followed him into the sitting room; a room full of sea and clouds and formal furniture, and there on a sofa lay Anna, propped by cushions and covered with a red blanket.

'She was so cold,' he said. He stood by the door, not wanting to get any nearer to his wife.

Cautiously Caroline crossed the room and stood by Anna, looking down at her. Her forehead was dark blue and one of her eyes was swollen. Caroline touched the side of her face with a finger and then put her hand on her thin shoulder. She was cold all right, but not . . . oh God . . . not . . .

'What happened? When . . . ?'

'She fell in the hall last night.'

'Last night? You mean to say—'

'I did not hit her. I was going up the stairs and she fell. She was running across the hall. I heard her fall. She tripped. Yes. I heard her. I just went on up the stairs. I thought . . . well, I was tired. I didn't want a scene and . . . I heard her fall. She called out but I just went on up to bed. Then, later, much later, five or six, I got up to go to the bathroom and all the lights were on and I looked down over the banisters and I saw her lying there. On the floor. In the hall. She had tripped over my coat. She could not be dead. Could she? No, no, of course she couldn't be. She called out. I heard her calling out. I just went on.'

'Where's the telephone?'

'What?'

'The telephone. Where's the fucking telephone? I must ring an ambulance.' She was startled by the shrillness of her own voice.

'An ambulance? What do you want an ambulance for? She tripped over this.' He was trailing the coat behind him and he shook it in her direction. 'Did I not tell you? She banged her head. She will be . . .'

'Just tell me where the telephone is. Please.'

He pointed across the hall, towards the door of his study. 'Telephone. In there on the table. There.'

He moved forlornly towards his wife, dragging the coat behind him.

As she hurried across the hall, she wondered should she keep him with her, under her eye. Just in case, just in case, she murmured the words to herself. Please don't let her be dead. Oh please. Nine nine nine. Must be the same. Nine nine nine. The phone was buried under a pile of papers. She picked up the receiver. She cleared her throat, must be clear, quite clear. She had never dialled nine nine nine before, a new experience. Her hand was shaking. Nine nine nine. Easy. She heard his steps shuffling across the hall. Nine nine nine, she pushed the buttons. Nine nine nine. Done. Behind her he coughed.

'Do you need fire, police or ambulance?'

'Yes. Yes,' she said. 'Please. Ambulance.'

'Can you give me the address please.'

'One Sorrento Terrace. An old lady has fallen.'

'One Sorrento Terrace. An ambulance is on its way. Do you need any help on the telephone?'

'No. Thanks.'

'Someone will be with you soon.'

'Thank you.' She put the telephone back.

'She wouldn't like that.' His voice was cross. She turned. He was standing in the doorway, struggling with the sleeves of his overcoat. He was punching them, shaking them as if he were fighting with someone. 'That old lady bit. She hated old lady. She did, does not consider herself to be old.'

'What are you doing with your coat?'

'I have to put it on. I may have to go somewhere with her.'

'You'd do better to get dressed. And put your . . . ummm . . .' She stopped.

He threw his coat on to the table.

'They will come,' he shouted at her. 'And take her away. Out there. God knows where. And maybe I will never find her again. If I'm upstairs. That is, putting on my clothes, that sort of thing. That takes time, you know. They may arrive at any moment.'

'I suggest you ring your sons.' She gestured at the phone.

'Later. When we know something or other. Yes. Then. Something or other.'

She heard the wail of an ambulance in the distance.

He picked up the coat and began to struggle with it once more. 'They fuss, you know. Fuss, fuss, fuss.'

'I'd better go and open the door, they'll be here at any minute.'

He pushed one arm into his coat and stood looking triumphantly at his hand as it appeared out at the bottom end of the sleeve.

She opened the door just as the ambulance drew up to

the kerb; a small dark man stepped out before the wheels had stopped turning.

'Here we are, missus,' he said in a cheerful voice.

'Yes, thank you. You've been very quick.'

'That's the name of the game. Where do we go, missus?'

'I'll show you. It's the ground floor. At least you won't have to ...'

Desmond began shouting in the hall. 'Do not let them in. Do not ... not I say ... do not ...'

She smiled anxiously at the ambulance man. 'Follow me. Don't pay any attention to him. He's a bit confused.'

'They'll take her. I'll never find her ...'

The driver got out of the cab and went round to the back of the ambulance. He opened the door.

'I'm just after you, Mick,' he called to his partner.

Desmond stood in the middle of the hall with one arm still in his coat.

'Everything will be all right,' she said to him as they hurried past him. Tears streaked his face.

'I don't want them to take her away.'

Caroline went through the sitting-room door.

'I don't really know what happened. She fell. He rang and told me that she had fallen.' She stood by the door and watched as the ambulance man stooped over the old woman. He touched her neck, her face and then delicately took her wrist between his fingers and held it for a while. He frowned. His companion bustled in with the stretcher.

'Is that your dad out there?' he asked as he passed Caroline.

'No.'

'He's not in great shape. What's the situation, Mick?' He put the stretcher on the floor and went over to his friend.

'She doesn't look too good. We'd better shift her asap.'

'Yep.'

He opened up the stretcher and unstrapped a blanket from it.

'Anything broken?'

Mick shook his head. 'She's bloody freezing.'

'Yep.'

'That's a nasty bang on her head.'

'Yep.'

Mick bent forward and gently wrapped the old lady in the blanket, then they both lifted her on to the stretcher. Caroline could see no sign of life, no breath, no stirring of the body.

'Is she . . . ?'

Mick made a little pout with his lips. 'She'll be OK, missus. We'll whisk her off now to Loughlinstown. She'll be OK.'

They hoisted up the stretcher and set off across the room. 'Will you folly?'

'Folly?'

'With yer man.'

They were crossing the hall. Caroline pattered after them. Desmond was still standing in the middle of the floor, looking dazed.

'Is she dead?'

'I don't think so.'

He pushed his arm back into the sleeve of his coat. 'I suppose they want me to go with them?'

'For God's sake, Desmond, go and put your clothes on.'

'Aye,' said Mick. 'Away you go and get dressed, there's a good lad. Then folly us. We're taking her to Loughlinstown. The sooner the better.'

Caroline opened the door and the two men manoeuvred the stretcher out and across the pavement and up the little ramp into the ambulance.

Mick closed the doors on himself and Anna. His companion turned to Anna.

'Is she your mother?'

Caroline shook her head. 'No relation. I hardly know them. I really can't work out why I'm here.'

'Well, whatever, if you'd get him up to the hospital sometime. He looks in poor shape himself.'

'They have two sons.'

'That's the ticket.'

With a little flick of the wrist, he turned, hopped into

the cab and was away, the siren sounding for a moment . . . goodbye, Caroline, it seemed to say. She went back into the house. He was still standing in the same place. Rooted. She touched him on the arm.

'Come. You must get dressed and then you must ring the boys and tell them about their mother.'

'Yes.' He didn't move. 'I suppose I should call them. I suppose it would be best if they knew where she was. Yes. It would be best if they knew that she is not going to die.' He shook himself, like a dog coming out of the sea. 'First. First. I must have coffee. You must have coffee. I have been so . . . so . . . We must both have coffee. After that I'll . . .' He dropped the coat on the floor and marched past her towards the kitchen, head up, shoulders back, left, right, fit as a fiddle.

She watched him and wondered whether to get out, run as fast as she could back to Notting Hill and never come back. The temptation was enormous. This is not my problem. Yes it is, you fool. You're here. You must deal with it. Slowly she followed him into the kitchen. He was filling the kettle, water splashed on to the floor beside him.

'I'll do that. You sit down.'

'Thank you, my dear. I do have to say that I am a little rattled by circumstances.'

He handed her the kettle and sat himself in a chair at the table. He took a handkerchief from the pocket of his dressing gown and rubbed at his face. She plugged in the kettle. He cleared his throat.

'I shot a man once. Yes. I remember that distinctly. I dream about that happening from time to time.' Unexpectedly he chuckled.

She did not want to hear his reminiscences.

'Where will I find a coffee pot?'

'It was in Austria, just after hostilities had ceased, like a day or two after. I—'

She banged on the counter with a fist. 'Desmond, just tell me where the coffee pot is. Please.'

He blinked at her, not hearing, not caring to hear. He continued to talk.

'That's what we used to say, never the war is over, always hostilities . . .'

She opened the cupboard in front of her. A row of coffee pots faced her. Jugs, a mini cona, two cafetières, a large espresso machine and two small ones. She took down one of the cafetières and looked for the coffee. She knew there was no point in asking him, his voice was droning on, presumably, she thought, about the man he said he'd killed in Austria.

'It was him or me, straight down the line, even though hostilities had ceased. I've never worked out yet whether I did the right thing or not. Sometimes I think it was all a dream. Well, nightmare, I suppose. There was so much blood. That startled me. I wasn't expecting that. Blood. Everywhere.'

'I'm making coffee. I don't want to hear all this stuff. It's too early in the morning. It can wait a while, can't it? Or never, maybe I never want to hear this story. I hate stories about death and blood. Why don't you go and ring the boys? That's what you ought to do.'

'I'll ring them in my own good time. I need to be calm when I ring them. I need some coffee.'

'It's coming.'

'Have you found the coffee?'

'It can't be far away.'

'I would have died had I not done it. That's the long and the short of it. Dead. He, the Nazi, would have shot me and none of my work, my better work, would have existed. Don't you think that most of my better work was written in those ten years after the war?'

'Found it.' She plucked a jar from the shelf and spooned some coffee into the coffee pot. 'I'm really not listening. My ears are closed. This coffee smells good.'

The kettle began to whisper.

'Do you like your milk hot or cold?'

'Cold will do. No. I think I'll drink it black. Sugar. I like quite a lot of sugar. I have a sweet tooth.' He began to pound with his fists on the table. 'Why has that bastard come back to visit me now?'

The kettle clicked and she poured the boiling water into the jug, the steamy aroma enveloped her. Carefully she placed the plunger on top of the pot and then searched for some cups.

'Not long now,' she said to him.

He paid her no heed. He was sunk deep into his own dreary thoughts, not about Anna, but about some distant German whom he thought he had killed. Just another figment, she thought. She pushed down the plunger.

'There was Abby too. Maybe I killed her.'

She poured out his coffee and carried it across the room. She banged it down on the table beside him.

'Look here, Desmond, there's one thing I'd like to say. You did not kill Anna. You did not hit Anna. You just went to bed and left her lying on the floor. That was unkind, but not criminal. They'll sort her out in the hospital. She'll be home in a day or two and you must stop dredging up all these old brutish deaths or you'll drive yourself mad. Now drink up your coffee and go and ring one of your sons.'

His hand was shaking as he raised the cup to his mouth. He took a tiny exploratory sip and then a larger one. He looked across the table at her and smiled.

'Of course you're right, my dear. Undoubtedly. I must say to you that I don't want it to be known abroad about the man I shot. I have spoken about this to no one.' He shook his head and took another drink from the cup. 'No one at all. You see, I have these tapes, I'm editing them all into mini broadcasts. I became a broadcasting man, you know. During the war that was. I enjoyed that medium. I thought it would be interesting to make a series of broadcasts of my life. My view of my life, rather than other people's view. They do invent, move the focus. Don't you find that? You do make good coffee, my dear. Excellent. I haven't spoken about Abby either, to anyone. Of course I know I didn't kill her intentionally, just my inattention. The decisions I made. When you look back at the important decisions you make in your life, it makes you shudder with alarm, how sometimes you don't seem to have given any thought to what you were doing at all. Inattention. Neglect. Years of my neglect killed her. I do think so. Of course she married someone else within weeks, you know, a man called Rory Beamish. They had a couple of children, but all the time she was pining away for me. She didn't love him. I should have married her, you know. She was the one of the three that I really loved and what did I do? I broke her heart. If the war hadn't happened I might have made a different decision. War is a terrible thing and yet there are those who say you'll never become a real man until you've experienced war. Fools. Savages. Am I talking too much? Am I rambling?' He stopped abruptly and stared at her. 'You disconcert me, my dear. You look at me as if you didn't believe a word I was saying. Anna thinks I am beginning to dote. I know by the way she looks at me, by the way she speaks to me. Of course I'm not, I just lead my life more and more on my tapes.' He drank some more coffee. 'If she were to die, I could not continue to live alone in this house.' He stared around him as if he was already a stranger in the room.

'She is not going to die. Get that into your head.'

He wasn't listening.

'I sometimes wonder if Pamela and I . . . no. That would be pure foolishness. She would rootle out all my secrets in a few days. She would connive and spy and make jokes. Wouldn't she? What do you think?'

'I don't really know . . .'

'Of course. How could you know?' He leaned back in his chair and looked up at the high, dark ceiling.

'What about the boys?' she asked. 'I'm sure—'

He laughed. 'They have their own lives to lead. They have full lives. They don't want parents, one or two parents, mixed up with their lives. They have work and women, drink and drugs, like everyone of their age. We would not be welcome in their lives. Times are very different now. The old are disregarded now, packed away in cupboards, like old useless clothes. Yes. We wouldn't welcome their lives either. Cars revving in the night, doors banging, parties of insubstantial young people we neither know nor like. Strangers dossing on our floors.' He shook his head violently.

'Why don't you pop upstairs and get dressed? You'll feel much more together when you come down. You're letting your imagination run away with you. We'll decide what to do when you come down again.'

'I feel like talking. I feel like talking to a person, not a machine. I'm tired of talking into a machine. Bored.'

He looked at her, his eyes pleading for something, she hadn't a clue what it might be. She reached her hand out towards him across the table and he clutched at it as if he were drowning.

'Please let me talk. After all, why did you come here? You thought you might trap me into telling you things that no one else knew, didn't you?'

'Not exactly. No. I never wanted to trap you into anything. Have some more coffee.'

'No.' He stood up slowly. 'I will go and dress myself. She usually puts my clothes out for me. The day's costume. But I suppose I can manage for myself.'

'I'm sure you can.'

He turned and walked wearily towards the door; he looked so old, much, much older than yesterday, a bundle of dying limbs dragging itself across the floor. At the door he turned back to her.

'Don't tidy up or anything like that. The foreign lady does that. She likes to do that, cleaning up after other people is her great pleasure.'

He left the room and she listened to him dragging himself across the hall and then up the stairs, past his father at the bend in the stairway and then up, dragging interminably up.

She poured herself another cup of coffee. The silence was heavy, a burden in her head, on her shoulders, pressing her down into the chair. What the hell have I let myself in for? Then she heard the shuffle of his feet in the room above her, she heard the taps turning and the sound of water running through the pipes. She heard footsteps outside in the street, the wheels of a car splashed through a puddle and she heard a dog bark.

She remembered that she was supposed to be having dinner with Pamela.

Was that Saturday or Sunday?

Was today Saturday or Sunday?

Was this all a figment of her imagination?

Gently she tapped the side of her face with her hand. Wake up. Please, Caroline, wake up.

A telephone by the cooker caught her eye. Reassured by the bumps and bangs upstairs, she went out into the hall and found her bag, she brought it back into the kitchen and dialled Pamela's number. After a long time a sleep-distorted voice answered.

'Who the hell?'

'I'm sorry. Did I wake you? I'm terribly . . .' She looked

at her watch; it was only quarter to eight.

'It's Saturday. Who the hell are you anyway?'

'Caroline.'

'Caroline who? I know hundreds of Carolines.'

'We met yesterday with Desmond Fitzmaurice. Caroline Wallace.'

'Oh yes. You. What do you want?'

'It's about Desmond actually. There's been an accident . . .'

The voice at the other end woke up. 'Is the poor old bugger dead?'

'No. But she is—'

'Dead?'

Was there a hint of laughter?

'No. I don't think so, but she's in hospital and he's a bit . . .'

'Where are you? What did you ring me for? What the hell do you think I can do? Hey.'

'I'm here in their house. He called me hours ago and I came. I called the ambulance. He was incapable of doing anything when I got here. He seems a bit . . . deranged. I don't know what to do.'

'So you woke me up.'

'Yes. I'm sorry. I don't know anyone else.'

'He has two perfectly good sons. Why didn't you wake them?'

'I tried to get him to call them, but he wouldn't.'

'Hmmm. Well, I don't know what you want me to do, but I'll give you one piece of advice. Get the number of one of those boys . . . men, I should say, it's many a long year since either of them has been a boy. Ring him up, tell him what has happened and then get the hell out. Go back to London or wherever it is you came from and forget us all.' She yawned somewhat noisily. 'I'm going to have to get up now and ready myself for whatever the day may bring. Thanks to your somewhat inopportune call. I will alert Ellie, when I'm dressed. Maybe she will dash round and scramble some eggs for her poor old dad. I think that's pretty unlikely, though, knowing the same lady, but you never can tell.' She gave a merry little laugh. 'If you are coming to dine tonight, bring the poor old bugger with you.'

'I think . . . perhaps . . .'

'Well, whatever. Buzz me. Let me know what's happening.'

She put down the receiver.

Caroline began to cry.

Damn.

She poked at her eyes with her fingers, but the tears just kept bursting out and running down her cheeks.

Hot tears.

Down her neck.

Splashing on to her shirt.

Damn.

She picked up the phone and punched out Herbert's number.

Damn.

He answered almost at once. She had a picture of him standing by the kitchen window with a cup of coffee steaming in his hand.

She stuttered his name through her tears.

'Caroline,' he said. 'What's up, my darling?'

'Herbert . . .'

She heard Desmond's shuffling feet crossing the hall and quickly put down the telephone. She picked up a napkin from the table and scrubbed at her face. His breath snuffled as he walked and she wished she could possibly be somewhere else.

He was a different man when he came into the room, upright and handsome. His white hair flopped agreeably on his forehead, his face was pink and shining from his facecloth. No bristles, no snot, just shining clean flesh. His teeth were in place. Round his neck he had tied a blue silk scarf and his trousers looked newly pressed.

'I must apologise,' he said, as he came through the door, 'for behaving in such an outrageous fashion. I am more myself now.' He walked over to the table, upright, like an old soldier, she thought. He picked up her hand and raised it to his lips. 'Dear lady, please forgive me. I was in shock. One cannot be blamed for what one does when one is in shock.'

He smiled most charmingly at her. 'I will now telephone Arthur, one of my boys. Yes. Arthur.' He dropped her hand and picked up the telephone, tapped a number and stood waiting with the receiver held a little way from his ear.

Caroline wondered whether to go or stay; stay, mumbled a little voice in her ear. She settled herself back into her chair and took a sip of coffee. It was cold. That almost made her cry again.

A voice squawked down the phone.

'Yes. Dear boy. Yes, yes. It is indeed. I'm sorry. I didn't intend... No. No. Nothing's the matter... well, your mother actually... She had a little fall. No. Nothing to do with me. I found her. Well... yes, in the hall. She had fallen. Yes. An hour or so ago. She had fallen... She was very cold. Yes. No. No. NO. I called the ambulance. Yes. It was the sensible thing to do. I thought so. She was very cold. Yes. They came. They've taken her to Loughlinstown. I thought that either you or Marcus might pop in and see how she is. I mean she'll be fine, but it would... Of course I'll go. A bit later on in the day I'll go. No. I'm all right. I can assure you of that, dear boy. Right as rain. No, I don't need... You'll do that. Good man. And tell her I'll be in la... and if you see a doctor or someone... let me know... quite... quite. It's in your hands... yes. Goodbye. Goodbye.'

He put down the telephone. 'I don't know why young people don't get up out of their bloody beds.'

'It's Saturday and anyway I don't suppose he's all that young. Is he?'

'Ha! He's younger than I am. Yes. I get up. She gets up.'

Caroline thought of Pamela. Pamela did not get up.

'But he'll go. He'll find out how she is. He'll deal with it all. He's more on the ball than Marcus. Marcus is a dreamer, always late, never known to make a decision. No. Never. Might be gay. It has crossed my mind. She would know. She knows that sort of thing. She wouldn't care if he were. I must say I'm rather old-fashioned about that sort of thing. Just a bit. Now, dear young lady, why don't we go into my study and do a little work? Get on with things. As I brought up the dead German, maybe I should explain. Make that little story clear?'

She was fed up with the whole business; she wanted to go home, she wanted to stand in front of the Lit. Ed. and say, do your own hack work in future. She wouldn't even mind being sacked.

'I think you—'

'Come.' It was a peremptory command. He marched out of the room, she rose and pattered after him.

'And of course Abby. I must clarify that situation also. Poor darling Abby. She was, you know, the love of my life.'

'Shouldn't you . . .'

He was searching through a box of tapes.

'I know this is very old-fashioned. The tape is a thing of

the past. One day, I mean to say before too long, I will get all this stuff on to disk, named and numbered, easy to find, easy to work with. Sit down. Make yourself comfortable. You see, I have been a man of many parts. Some more interesting than others. Some, though I say it myself, of great importance, and yet I have never been cherished for my creativity. I would like this, my country, to cherish me. Before I die. What use is it if it comes after death? I want the accolades now. Is that crass? Hey? What do you think, dear lady?'

'I...'

'I ramble on. I ramble on. Sometimes I think I detect a touch of almost dementia. Does it seem like that to you? Have I left my self-renovation too late? I want you to ... ah ... here it is.' He held a tape up for her to see. He jiggled it up and down in front of her eyes. He stared at it for quite a long time. 'It is years since I played it. I suddenly feel quite nervous.'

'Are you sure you want to play it to me?'

He was fixing it into the tape player.

'It saves me having to talk so much. I can listen in silence. That will renew the whole scene. It is only a scene. Not long. No. It is not long. You don't need to worry about the length. It is for me a potent point in my life. As, indeed, was she, Abby. Potent, meaningful. She had a child, you know, not long after marrying Beamish. They went to America, almost immediately. Her cousin told me about the child. For years I did wonder, on and off. I felt unbearably sad when I thought of her, when I thought of the child, but as the years passed I realised it probably was not my child and the weight of sadness lifted. That wonderful woman died an age ago, well before her time, as I said before, of my inattention.'

Like hell she did, thought Caroline to herself.

He fiddled with the tape machine, his hands trembling.

'Perhaps,' said Caroline hopefully, 'you should play it to yourself. Alone. See what you think.'

'Sit.' He pointed to the armchair by the window.

She sat down. In the garden next door a child in pyjamas was throwing a ball for a dog. Both of them were giving small inarticulate cries of joy. Beyond them, the sea was striped with glittering ripples and the sun was rising orange in the sky. He continued fiddling with the tape machine, all fingers and thumbs, then suddenly he threw himself down into his chair, leaned back and closed his eyes. The machine whirred for such a long time that Caroline thought it wasn't going to work. Someone called to the child in the garden next door and he and the dog galloped into the house for their breakfast. There was a long sigh from the tape machine.

How many days, weeks, months since I killed that man?
 A long time.

Years, in fact. Many years.

Yet nowadays I dream of him. He inhabits the darker corners of my life. I sometimes raise my eyes from the keyboard, or a book that I may be reading and he is there, across the table in the evening darkness, his face and hands pale, his hair lank and slightly golden in colour. I hear his voice from time to time, low and precise, speaking immaculate English, as I walk on the beach below my house, or put the key in the ignition of my car.

I push these unwanted visitations away. I don't want this spectre in my life.

He was a German.

He was the enemy. Albeit defeated, still the enemy.

The scene, as I call it, was in the Austrian Alps. Phaeton stopped the jeep at the top of a valley and we sat looking down towards a cluster of houses, just beginning to light up for the evening. The sun was setting, casting blackness over half the valley. A few wisps of smoke waved from the chimneys. That made me smile. Some people were burning their furniture, their tables and chairs, chopping up their armoires and their grandfather clocks and feeding them into their cooking stoves.

Yes. I smiled at that thought.

Hostilities had ceased.

They had not won the war and so desperation and degradation had set in.

Yes.

That made me smile.

We sat, he in his car and Phaeton and I in the jeep, and stared down the valley at the peaceful scene below us. Mountains, pine trees and a stream that curled its way through the fields and past the houses to goodness knows where.

Hostilities had ceased.

The world that yesterday had been at war was now at peace; well, some of it, anyway.

I laughed.

I rolled down the window of the jeep and laughed again, throwing my laughter in his direction. He did not stir. He just continued to sit staring down the valley at the drifting smoke and the stream that wound to God knows where. I bet he knew. He had the look of a scholarly man, a man who would know most things. He wore no hat and his hair dangled on his forehead in pale wisps, his hands rested on the steering wheel, there was a shine on his cheeks that maybe came from tears. I couldn't be sure. I opened the door of the jeep and got out. A gentle breeze was blowing up the valley.

'Where are you off to?' asked Phaeton.

The gun was in the pocket of my greatcoat, not, I knew, the best place to keep a gun, but there it was anyway, unused.

'I'm just going to have a few words with . . .' I nodded towards the other car, a dark green Adler.

'Hostilities have ceased,' said Phaeton.

It was a stolen gun that I had taken from a prisoner and kept, just, as I said to myself, in case . . .

'Thank you for those words.' I stepped away from him towards the dark green Adler.

I knocked on the window of his car.

He paid me no attention. In fact I wondered if he were dead. I knocked again and slowly he turned his grey eyes towards me. He took a hand from the steering wheel and rolled down the window.

'Yes?'

'I'd like to talk to you. Just for a few minutes.'

'You may talk for as long as you wish.' His voice was indifferent, his accent flawless.

'May I get in the car with you?'

'No.'

He turned his eyes back once more to the valley. I wondered for a moment what I should do; leave the man to his bruising thoughts or carry through my own probably rather stupid plan.

'What are you staring at?'

'That is none of your business.'

'Just answer the question.'

'Nichts. Nothing.'

There was a silence between us.

'In case of misunderstanding, by nothing I mean blackness, lack of hope, living death. Golden lads and girls all must, as chimney sweepers come to dust.'

'Elegy for a dead Führer?'

'You could say that, or a dead civilisation.'

'I'm sure he would have preferred a few well-chosen words from a German poet.'

'You, sir, would not have the faintest idea what he would or would not have preferred. Shakespeare is not the sole property of the English.'

'There are a great number of people who wouldn't agree with you.'

'Art, sir, is universal.'

'You think your Führer believed that?'

He bowed his head. 'Our Führer, sir, believed in art and beauty, in purity, our purity as a race. Had we been victorious, had you listened to us, had you believed in what we were saying to you before all this happened, we could have swept Europe clean. Yes. He would have led us pure and free to the steps of God's throne. We would all have been saved.'

'My goodness, what a lot of bullshit you do have in your head.'

He turned and stared at me, his eyes full of hatred.

'I presume it is the victor's right to be arrogant, if he so wishes, but one day you will realise that we were right. If you had listened to us, if you had only listened, none of this need have happened and Europe would have been clean and free, a place of delight and harmony, instead of . . .' He waved his hand towards the village beneath us. 'We have become beasts. You and yours are beasts. I wish you joy of your victory. The law of the jungle will prevail, just you wait and see.'

Then I took the gun from my coat pocket and shot him in the head.

It was such an easy thing to do. I was surprised. It was something that I had never done before, something that I hope never to do again.

There was an awful lot of blood.

I had not thought about blood.

I had forgotten its colour, its consistency, its smell. I felt it trickling down my face. His blood. The whole world seemed to be smeared with blood. His blood. He leant against the door of the car, looking so small and surprised and bloody. For a moment only I wished that I hadn't shot him.

Phaeton was suddenly there by my side with a handful of cloths. I stood quite still while he rubbed at my head and face and my right hand. He took off my jacket and threw it into the back of the jeep, then he wrapped the gun in the bloodied cloths and threw them over the edge of the valley.

'Hostilities have ceased,' he said once more. 'But you done good.'

We drove in silence back to our billets.

The voice stopped. The tape whirred for another moment or two and then clicked off.

Desmond leant forward in his chair; his eyes were shining as he stared into Caroline's face.

She didn't know what to say; she felt her face going red. She put a hand up and touched her cheek, it was burning hot.

'That was, of course, fiction.'

He frowned. 'Certainly not. I killed that man. That Nazi. I crossed the road to his car and I shot him. I brought the gun with me. I wanted to kill a German, preferably a Nazi, and I did.'

'I don't believe you. Why would you do such a frightful thing? I mean—'

'You don't know what you're talking about. You could not begin to understand about men, about war, about heroes—'

'Hang on a second. This isn't a story about heroes. This is a pathetic story, whether it's true or false. A horrible, dirty little made-up tale and I wish you hadn't told it to me.'

He got up slowly from his chair and walked over to the window, he stood and stared down at the sea. He leant a shoulder against the shutters. Everything about him drooped. She wondered for a moment if he had tried to kill Anna. Don't be daft, she muttered in her head, of course he didn't. She tripped over his coat and banged her head on the floor. Accident, it's called.

Yeah.

Accident.

He was talking on.

'Heroes dig into life. They discover the filth and continue to live. They can sing. Look at Ulysses or ... or Hamlet. Look at Lear. They both had to come to grips with the reality of living. Not the sublime life. There is no sublime life, no matter what the poets and writers say. Never sublime. There is pain and suffering, lies and plots, death ... then of course it's over. Kaput, done. But of course you know such things. We all know such things. We just avoid thinking about them. Don't we?'

'I don't know what you're going on about.'

'Of course you do. I murdered that German. Twenty-four hours earlier and it wouldn't have been murder, but hostilities had ceased and abracadabra, it was. I had never drawn blood. For five years I had been a watcher, a recorder, noble of course, quite noble, but quite, quite unreal. So, I had to do it and in a way I suppose I was lucky, I happened to hit on a Nazi. So I can consider that I did a bit of world cleansing. My own little bit, my private bit. And now I'm giving you this story as a present. What, I wonder, will you do with it?'

Before she could answer, the doorbell rang.

He shook himself, as a dog does when it comes out of the sea.

'My goodness,' he said and stared at her. 'I wonder who that can be.'

She made no attempt to get up. He could bloody well answer his own doorbell, she thought.

'I wonder.' He turned from the window and moved across the room. He walked heavily, but with confidence.

Whoever was outside the door put his finger on the bell and kept it there.

She heard the sound of the door being opened and voices speaking. The door was closed and the voices and the sound of steps crossed the hall.

Desmond came first into the room, followed, almost pushed, by a blond man, small, slightly hunched, who looked as if he had just fallen out of bed.

'This is Arthur, my . . . ahh . . . son. Yes. Arthur.'

Caroline got to her feet. 'How do you do?'

'Caroline.' Desmond waved his hand in her direction as he said her name.

Arthur nodded at her. He hadn't shaved nor had he combed his hair, but then it was Saturday and there was a crisis on, she thought. They all looked at each other and the gulls outside the window began their wheeling and crying.

How I would love to be translated back to Notting Hill, she thought.

Desmond's attention drifted towards the birds.

'What's going on?' Arthur asked her fretfully. 'What are you doing here? Where's my mother? What the hell is going on?'

'He rang me and I came. I was asleep. I didn't know what else to do. He sounded—'

'I know how he sounded. Confused, as usual, I understand that, but who are you? Why did he ring you?'

'The mackerel are gathering again. Look at the birds.'

The old man's eyes were fixed on the wheeling, crying birds. There must have been thirty of them, at least. Wheeling, wheeling, waiting to swoop, to dive, to rise again, each holding in its beak the glittering prize.

'I always wonder why the fish keep coming back and back here where only death awaits them.' He laughed. 'Only death. I suppose you could say the same thing for all of us. Just the other side of this door, round this corner or the next one. Or of course maybe not. It is waiting somewhere.'

He put his two spread-out hands on the window and bent forward, not taking his eyes from the birds.

'What lures them back to this spot? The fish I mean.'

'Why did he ring you? Why did he not ring me? Or Marcus? Excuse me for asking, why you?'

'I don't know any more than you do. I have met your father twice. I'm over here to write a piece about him. I haven't the foggiest idea what is going on. Your mother is in a place called . . . called . . .' She hesitated over the name.

'Loughlinstown.' The old man didn't turn from the window as he spoke.

'Is she all right? You said she had a fall. How did she fall? Father. Desmond. Come away from the window and talk to me.'

The birds had begun to dive; first one went and then quickly after, a cascade of gulls sprayed from the sky. Caroline watched, fascinated.

'Desmond!'

The old man sighed and turned from the window.

'Yes, Arthur?'

Behind him a bird rose, hefted by the wind, its wings stretched out but unmoving, in its beak a desperate flash of silver. Another and then another and the wind lifted them up above the roofs and the trees and the hill.

'As I said, I didn't see her fall. I didn't hear her calling out. I must have been asleep when it happened. I presumed she had come upstairs straight after me, as she usually does. I am telling you the truth. The unvarnished truth. Why on earth would I lie to you about such a thing?'

'Hmmmm,' said his son.

'When I came down this morning, I just found her there, stretched out. There on the floor. I touched her. Yes. I bent down and touched her. I called her name out. She was so cold. I thought for a moment ... well, luckily they say she's ... Luckily. I was really worried for a—'

'Why didn't you ring me? Or Marcus?'

'It was so early. Too early, I felt, to ... well. I had Caroline's number at hand. So I rang her. And she came. That was the easiest thing to do. I pulled her into the sitting room and put her on the sofa. I got a rug. I didn't want her to stay as cold as she was. She was heavier than I thought possible. Dead ... um ... weight. But I managed.'

Arthur turned and stared at Caroline.

'I know nothing. He sounded distressed and so I came. Pretty reluctantly, I do have to say. What else could I have done?'

'Why didn't you go with her to the hospital?'

Desmond thought for a moment, he frowned and pulled at his lip with a finger.

'Should I have gone with her? No one ever suggested that I should go.'

'He wasn't dressed,' said Caroline. 'They would have had

to wait while he got dressed. It seemed best to let them take her as fast as possible. I reckon you should go there now, as quickly as you can, and find out how she is and ring your father and let him know. Let them know at the hospital that she has relatives who care about her.'

'What a splendid idea. Perfectly splendid. Yes, you go, dear boy, and then later I could pop across with Phaeton and bring her something to read and . . . and some grapes. Later.' He turned back almost cheerfully to the window. 'Birds,' he said.

'Fuck the shagging birds,' said his son.

'There is no call . . .' said his father and then stopped. 'I presume you came in your motor car. Of course you did. You pop along then, dear boy. Off you go and see your mother. I have some work I must do, now that I have Caroline here, and then I will gather myself together. Yes.'

'Supposing she says that you hit her. You knocked her to the floor.'

'She won't say anything of the kind. I have told you what happened. I didn't as much as raise a hand to her.' His voice rose and his hands began to shake. 'That is a most preposterous suggestion. Preposterous. You have hurt me to the quick.'

The younger man frowned and looked down at the floor, his face went a little red.

'I seem to remember—'

'There is nothing to remember. I know your mother has falsely accused me of striking her. That was a gross lie, as well you know. I may have brandished my fist in her direction, but I have never hit her, never.'

'She rang the police. She told the police you hit her with your walking stick.'

'Hysteria, and of course a spot of drink.' He looked apologetically towards Caroline. 'I am sorry that you should be involved in such a—'

'You broke her bloody arm.' Arthur turned on his heel and left the room.

'An unseemly . . .'

They stood silently, each looking out of the window, until they heard the hall door bang. Desmond put out a hand and steadied himself on the back of his big chair.

'I am so sorry.' He repeated the words, his voice was grey. A cloud blew across the sun and everything became grey; the birds had all gone and only a little wind rippled the surface of the water.

I could go now, she thought to herself. He is not my problem, this accident is not my problem. His sons are alerted.

I could go.

Pick up my coat and march out the door.

Never, ever see him again.

Nor his birds.

Nor his wives.

One and two.

Nor listen to his tapes.

He was talking to her, peevishly, she thought, by the look on his face.

'. . . they take their mother's side. Whatever occurs. Both of them. Usually quite unjustifiably. Do sit down. You look as if you're about to take off. Make yourself comfortable. Do, please. Do.' He waved a hand towards the chair and then settled himself into his own one. Snuggling his bottom back among the cushions.

'I think I was a good father. I played games with them.' He searched back into his memory, frowning slightly as he did so. 'I took them to the zoo. I never took Ellie to the zoo, but I did the boys. Yes, and the circus. I remember taking them to Fossett's Circus, several times . . . and the Gaiety Pantomime. We used to take a box and they would ask their pals to come along. They enjoyed that. They all had ice cream in the interval. I did lots of things with them. Family sort of things. I was not a neglectful father.

'Anna occupied herself completely with them. She was a really good mother, better than . . . the other. Caring, she was caring. I cared too. When they were small, I bounced them on my knee. I sang songs to them. I played peepbo.' He put his hands up in front of his face and then pulled them away, making roguish eyes at her as he did so. 'I taught them to swim...maybe no, maybe that was their mother, now I come to think of it. I sat through those interminable concerts at their school, and the buggers end up hating me.'

'I don't suppose they hate you.'

'They show no regard for me. They have forgotten all those days. I loved my mother. I cried for months after she died. All times of the day or night I would find myself suddenly weeping. I longed and longed for her still to be there in my life. I needed to hear the sound of her voice, feel her hand on my shoulder, the powdery smell she had when she leaned towards me. She didn't like Pamela.' He laughed suddenly. 'Pamela did not like her. Oh no. Indeed she did not. I could tell you such stories...'

He shut his eyes and she wondered if he had fallen asleep.

'I'm sure they don't hate you. They're just in awe of you. Perhaps. That puts people at a disadvantage. Perhaps they think you're not very nice to their mother. That might make them angry.'

'Mother.' His voice was mournful, like some lonely night-time bird calling. 'You know, my dear, she used to type my work for me. I would speak the words, walk up and down the room. She would say, each day, "You'll wear a hole in the carpet with your marching up and down." And she would tap assiduously at her machine. Dictating, I believe it's called. I dictated, she tapped. I liked dictating, maybe that's why I made all these tapes. My secret tapes.' He burst for a moment into song. '"Daddy's on the railway, don't be afraid. Daddy knows what he is doing, said the little maid." She used to sing that.'

He looked keenly at her, waiting for some response. She shook her head. She didn't know what else to do.

'Did your father sing to you as well?' she asked him after a long silence.

'My father was quite austere.'

'Did he love you?'

'Austere people can love.'

'I apologise. I didn't mean to—'

'He played games, tennis, golf, cricket, he was a good bowler. Those were his frivolities, not singing songs to his child. He was a man's man. Sometimes he would pat my head. We loved him. Mother and I. We respected him. He was a kind and generous man. Now, suppose I were to play you another tape?'

'Is this a good time? Should you not be going to the hospital? Arranging things with your . . . um . . . driver? She will be waiting to see you.'

'Someone will ring me. I must just sit here and wait until that moment. For God's sake, woman, I don't want to go and see her. I hate hospitals. She may be lying there with her head full of accusations. Yes. I see by your face that you hate what I'm saying. I'll go. Of course I'll go, but if you want to know the truth, which I can't say to anyone except you, I don't care if she lives or dies. I did not hit her. But I don't care. I will go when someone rings me. Yes. I will. I did not hit her.'

'I believe you.'

'Will she die?'

'Oh, for God's sake.'

'Do you think she'll die?'

She didn't answer.

'She's no spring chicken. Ten years younger than I am. She was so pretty. Still is. Don't you think? And witty. She can make you roar with laughter. Pamela never cared much for sex, you know, but Anna . . . was otherwise. I think what they now call hot. Yes. She was very, very hot. And she loved me. I was never sure whether Pamela did or not. I don't think Pamela respected men.'

Caroline laughed. 'Come, come,' she said.

He looked affronted. 'Then, in those days, women respected men. Anna's eyes were bright with anticipation when they looked at me. Joyful anticipation and, of course, respect. Pamela always looked as if she had something else on her mind, I was not her sole object.'

'Did you want to be her sole object?'

'Of course. That was what my mother had taught me. And you may laugh, young woman. Who in this world do you respect?'

'You have to earn it.'

'And don't you think I have?'

'Yes, of course. As a writer, yes, of course ... but ...'

'Not as a person?'

'I don't know you. I only know the bits and pieces you've told me, and I don't think I believe them.'

'I'll play you one more tape ...'

'No.'

He looked surprised.

'I'll only play you one.' He rummaged in the box. 'Just one. You see, this woman is the woman I really should have married. I should have waited for her to arrive in my life. One is always told that the right person is there moving slowly in your direction, but you never believe that sort of rubbish. In this case it was right. I should have waited. Are you writing a book about me?'

'No. I told you what I'm doing, I am stirring up interest in you. That's all. My editor seems to think that your work is worth resurrecting. I don't even know why she picked on me to do this. I'm going to have to spend weeks reading everything you wrote. Bad as well as magnificent.'

'I would have you know that I was translated into twenty languages. Now I will play you just one,' he murmured, and rummaged on, his hands delving in the box. 'Fifty years ago. Must be. Almost fifty anyway.' He gave a little laugh. 'I remember her as if she had just gone out that door, every gesture, every bend of her head, every laugh, every breath she breathed. She ran away to America, you know. After that Rory chap, when she realised that Anna was pregnant. And I never saw her again. She never wrote me a letter or telephoned. All through the war, not a sound. She could have been dead. I used to dream about her, she was always coming towards me with her arms open and then ... just before she reached me she would vanish and I would be alone again. It was all very hard to bear.'

'Poor you.' Caroline muttered the words under her breath. 'What ... umm ... about Pamela?' she asked aloud.

'What about Pamela?'

'Well ... didn't she have a point of view? After all ...'

'Threw me out. Metaphorically changed the locks. Went to see Anna and screamed at her about stealing other people's husbands, suggested she should go to England and have an abortion. She reduced poor Anna to a sobbing wreck and said she never wanted to see me again. She was up to her ears in *Troilus and Cressida* and she felt very hard done by.'

'I don't blame her.'

'A good production, I do have to say. It's a play I don't like much. Definitely not one of the master's best, but she did a season of oddities, *Pericles, Timon of Athens, L L L,* plays she said no one in Dublin would ever see if she didn't put them on. The whole season was a surprising success. It was just before the war started. Yes. We got our timing a bit wrong. She acted a bit rough, though. She ordered a removal firm to come and take all my things out of the house and dump them at my mother's front door. I mean to say. She knew as well as I did that my mother knew nothing about any of this at all. It was a mean and unkind thing to do . . . It took some forgiving, I can tell you.'

'Your wife was working her guts out and you were running two other women and you . . .'

'Hey, hey, Pamela knew nothing about Abby.'

'. . . complain about Pamela being mean and unkind.'

'Anna didn't know about Abby either.'

He sounded triumphant, she thought, like a very clever operator.

'And what did your loving mother have to say?'

'Well, she never liked Pamela, so her heart wasn't broken when she found out, but she loathed the notion of divorce, sin, all that sort of thing. She was a believer in good and evil. I think she prayed for me quite a lot. Of course she was very pleased that the baby, when it arrived, was a boy. The war, though, made her more concerned for my bodily survival, she forgot her problems with my soul. And then the poor old dear died. I was sorry to have caused her grief. I do think if Pamela hadn't been so precipitate I could have smoothed things over for her. I would have let her know in a gentle way. She was old, they ordered things better in her youth. She would have liked me to be perfect, but she forgave my imperfections. Yes.'

'Oh, for heaven's sake—'

'No need to say another word. I see the disapproval on your face. Writ clear. Women are such disapprovers.'

'Of hypocrites. Yes. Of lying toads, yes.'

'Dear lady, such words of venom are uncalled for. Just because I'm telling you some of my secrets ... some of my—'

'Listen to me. I don't want to hear your secrets, or your fairy tales. I'll probably be sacked for being an inadequate hack, but that's too bad. I'm going to make us a cup of coffee. You're going to ring your taxi man and he will take you to the hospital and then I'm going home, back to London. To my normality. Get it?'

He stared at her, puzzled by her anger.

'But me? You can't leave me. I can't be left ...'

'You have two sons, a daughter, two wives, a cleaning lady and I don't know how many other people in your life. You can bloody well ring up one of them to come and hold your hand and listen to your stories.'

She got up from her chair and moved towards the door. He waved the tape at her.

'No.'

She stamped her way across the hall and back into the

kitchen. She heard the whirr of the tape machine and then his voice beginning to speak. She filled the kettle with water and washed the coffee pot. She knew she couldn't leave him on his own, but the moment the blinking son . . . what was his name? She searched in her brain. Arthur? Yes. She would go. Yes. The moment he rings. For God's sake, the moment anyone rings. Arthur. But maybe he wouldn't ring. Maybe no one would ever ring. Maybe she would be here forever.

Don't be such an ass, she said to herself. Arthur. She put a lot of coffee in the pot. Should she ring Pamela? Ask her to come round, hold the fort? But then suppose if she did and Anna were to come home with Arthur? Ructions. Yes. Wait. Just be calm. Don't panic. Some really strong coffee would pull her together. And him. He would become smooth and charming. He would assure her that he could manage on his own. She must go. Yes. Go. He would be fine. Absolutely fine. There was nothing to worry about.

The kettle boiled and she poured the water into the pot. Her face was enveloped in a rush of steam. She heard his shuffling footsteps coming into the room and wondered why he sometimes walked upright, lifting his feet from the floor like a younger man, and sometimes didn't seem to be able to manage to do this at all. He seemed to whisk old age on and off himself like an actor changing his costume.

'The coffee's made,' she said cheerfully.

He pulled out a chair and sat down at the kitchen table.

'You won't leave me, will you?'

'Milk or black?'

He ignored the question.

'I feel unwell. My head is bursting.'

She poured him a mug of coffee and put it beside him on the table. She took the milk jug from the fridge and put it beside the mug.

'I want you to tell me why you killed that German.' She poured some coffee for herself and sat down beside him.

'German?'

'Whatever he was. That man. You know who I mean.'

'The enemy. You mean the enemy?'

'You know perfectly well who I mean.'

'I don't know why you're asking.'

'I want to know. The war was over. You were anyway a noncombatant. You should not have had a weapon in your pocket. You had no right to kill him.'

The old man laughed.

'Right. You talk about right. Rights don't come into it. Pass me the sugar.' He spooned three spoonsful into his mug. 'Did you never hear of Auschwitz, of Belsen, Buchenwald, the dead, the mutilated, the tortured, in the name of cleansing the world. Well, as I told you before, I did my bit of cleansing too. No one had let me do it while the war was on, but the moment hostilities ceased, who was to stop me?' He looked up at her, triumphantly. 'I could have gone on the rampage and killed quite a lot of the enemy that day and no one would have said boo to me. No one would have noticed. But I didn't, I killed that weasel and I threw the gun away. What more do you want me to tell you?'

'Why do you have to tell the world now? Why don't you just leave the whole thing alone? Why tell me?'

He stirred his coffee for a moment and then scratched the top of his head.

'Perhaps . . .' He stopped and took a sip from his cup. 'Perhaps it is because he seems to have moved in with me. I don't like the feeling that he could be around the next corner, or sitting across the table. I remembered his face, suddenly, in the last few weeks. It was a face that I had totally forgotten. Now it appears beside me all the time. I don't like that. I thought I might be able to . . .' He took another drink and swished the liquid round inside his mouth. 'Yes,' he said eventually. 'Exorcise him in some way, if I told someone. I hoped to eliminate him from my life.'

He looked pathetically at her.

'You see, he is haunting me . . . even in Phaeton's car the other night he was there, sitting in the back seat, smiling. I nearly told Phaeton then, but I didn't think he would be the right person to help me.'

'Anna . . .'

'No.' He shouted the word at her. 'For heaven's sake, no. She'd have me in a nursing home in a minute. Last person to tell. Last, last person. Anyway, she may be dead.'

There was a long silence.

'Will you help me?' he asked at last.

'What on earth do you think I can do? You've got a little madness inside your head, that's all it is. Look, your son will be ringing you. Tell him about this. Ask him to come and talk to you. I'm sure he will be helpful.'

The old man shook his head. 'I have no friends left.'

'Drink up your coffee.'

He pushed his cup away. 'No one to talk to. Except my machine. Nowadays it makes strange noises, it moans and whines. Occasionally it won't start. What will I do if it gives up altogether?'

'Buy a new one.'

'I am not handy with these modern gadgets.'

The air was stale and despondent. Caroline wondered how long it had been since anyone had opened the window. Even out in the street nothing moved or sounded, there was only the distant drone of a plane and she longed to be on it, wherever it was going.

'My typewriter is almost fifty years old. I used it during the war, actually in the Western Desert. You have to beat the keys. That's what I'm used to. Nowadays you barely need to touch them, I find that hard to get used to. I don't have that feather-light touch. Patter, patter.' He ran his fingers over the table top. 'Patter, patter.' He smiled almost flirtatiously up at her. 'I like you. Do you like me? Or, or, or, or do you not?'

She blushed, embarrassed by his question. She didn't say anything. She drank some coffee and suddenly the doorbell rang.

'I wonder who that can be,' said the old man, not moving.

'Why don't you go and see?'

The idea surprised him, but after a moment he heaved himself to his feet and left the room.

She poured herself some more coffee, she looked at her watch, ten o'clock. God, it felt as if a whole day was almost over. She heard voices, a little rush of a shout from Desmond. She wondered if everything was all right. The door banged and the voices became more substantial. There was a woman, that she could make out. Then another little shout from Desmond and they came in through the door, Desmond, Anna and Arthur.

'You see,' said Desmond. 'She's back. The dear little queen of my life is home once more.' He was holding Anna by the hand. She had a rug wrapped round her shoulders, which trailed behind her across the floor.

'I mean to say, the moment Arthur appeared, I knew I must come home, so the dear boy dealt with all the doctors and matrons and red tape and all. Everything.' She sat down and threw the rug back from her shoulders. 'So here I am. I smell coffee. I have to go to bed. I promised them all that I would go to bed. I am exhausted. Hospital is so exhausting.'

Arthur was standing just inside the door. He looked exhausted too.

'She was on a trolley. Just plonked. In this long passage. Full of people on trolleys.'

'I did say to them that we had insurance, but no one had time to listen to me. Otherwise I might have been in a bed, in a room of my own. They simply did not listen. So he kidnapped me, didn't you, darling. If Arthur hadn't come along, I'd still be there on that bloody trolley. I know I haven't drunk coffee for years, but I would love some now. I'd love some coffee and a boiled egg and Arthur, darling, what about you? You haven't had any breakfast. What the hell are *you* doing here?' She turned her attention to Caroline. Sparks seemed to shoot from her eyes as she spoke.

'Well...'

'She came at my command. It was so good of her. I got her out of bed. I didn't know what to do when I found you there. Lying on the floor. My mind became a complete blank. Complete and utter. Hers was the first name that popped into my mind. Strange that. I carried you into the drawing room and wrapped you in a rug. You were so cold, my darling, I thought...' He stopped. He thought the better of it. He chewed at his lip. Everyone looked at him for a moment. He shook his head.

'A boiled egg and toast,' she said.

'Quite.' He looked towards Caroline.

She got to her feet.

'I must go,' she said. The words surprised her, they were not what she thought she was going to say. 'Yes. I must go. Now that everything is settled. I'm so glad you're all right. No ill effects.'

Anna interrupted her. 'They said I must go to bed. At once. Bed. Keep warm, lots of hot drinks. Didn't they?'

Arthur nodded gloomily.

'So . . . if you could ring for a taxi for—'

'My shoulder is badly bruised. All colours of the rainbow. The doctor wondered how that happened.'

'There's no point in looking at me. I did not touch you. You know that, woman. I did not lay one finger on you. You fell. You tripped over my coat.'

'Father—'

'I don't want to hear a word from you. You always side with your mother. You always believe every word she says. You swallow her lies, hook, line and sinker.' He turned to Caroline. 'Bring her up and put her to bed. I'll make her a nice hot cup of coffee.'

'No,' said Caroline. 'I won't. I'm going home. Now, this moment. If you won't get me a taxi, I'll walk to the bus. I've had enough of the lot of you. She can put herself to bed, and you can throw all those tapes of yours away. I don't know whether he pushed you or not and I don't care. All I say is fuck the lot of you, fuck my editor, fuck your books and plays, fuck this house and the birds and the fish and all eccentric Irish people.'

She walked across the room and out into the hall, leaving a dark silence behind her. Her bag was on the chair in the hall where she had left it when she arrived. As she picked it up, the silence in the kitchen was broken.

'What an extraordinary woman,' said Anna.

Caroline stood for a moment on the doorstep. The same dog came down the street and gave a sharp bark when it came to its own door, the same palm trees rustled across the road. The sky was blue and a bird wheeled lazily overhead.

Perhaps, she thought irrelevantly to herself as she began to walk towards Dalkey, we might be able to adopt a child. Two. Two. We'd have to adopt two. One child is a lonely thing, could turn out to be a lonely and eccentric adult, unable to work out truth from fiction.

She walked quicker. Behind her the dog barked again. By the time she got to the corner, she was running, her bag slapping against her left leg.

We must get on to that right away.

Yes. That's what we must do. The moment I get home.

Back home to Notting Hill.

✳   ✳   ✳

The magnolia in our front garden was in full flower when I arrived back from my trip to Dublin. A slight breeze was blowing down the road as I opened the gate and the big creamy flowers twitched and seemed to bow in my direction. I was delighted. I bowed back. I smiled graciously and I lifted my hand in a regal wave.

It was at that moment as I raised my hand to acknowledge their greeting that the thought came into my mind that I should try to write about what had happened over the last three days; just for myself, it would be nothing that I would give to the Lit. Ed. Possibly at some time in the future I might let Herbert read it, but I expect he might disapprove of my somewhat messy inaction, I might just keep it to myself, rather like Desmond's tapes, a memory of things past. I really do like to keep things simple.